BLOODLINES
AND OTHER STORIES

BLOODLINES
AND OTHER STORIES

Joyce Russell

MERCIER PRESS
IRISH PUBLISHER – IRISH STORY

MERCIER PRESS
Cork
www.mercierpress.ie

© Joyce Russell, 2012

ISBN: 978 1 78117 065 6

10 9 8 7 6 5 4 3 2 1

A CIP record for this title is available from the British Library

Printed and bound in the EU.

For Ben

CONTENTS

We All Fall Down   9

Changes of Light   22

Bloodlines   34

High Nellie and the Far Horizon   48

Comparable, Identical, One and the Same   65

Precious Little   72

Knocking Down the Nails   92

A Fair Trade   106

Fishing for Dreams   124

Every Cloud   132

Blood Red   141

Crying for Worms   151

Light, Thought and Evelyn   162

Least Said   175

Rose Petal Blues   190

Walking Backwards   200

Author's Note   218

Acknowledgements   219

WE ALL FALL DOWN

A fox can see well at night, but I can't. I've tried. Believe me! I've practised staring at the side of the barn wall, trying to read the words my brother scratched there years ago. In full daylight they say: 'I hate you all.' But as the sun fades and the last red glow flickers through the trees, they become tall, thin scratches: a tally of some sort that was never completed, never struck through.

There should be comfort in darkness because then the words are hidden, but some things don't hide, they lurk, waiting to spring out. And some things don't have to be seen at all: you just always know they are there.

I'd got off the school bus three stops early. Mr Mac, our driver, looked worried.

'Shouldn't you be getting home Kate?' he'd said. 'There's nothing more you can do between here and there.'

He was wrong, of course. There was plenty to do.

Like: watching the sun set, until it looked like the end of a fire left burning on the hill.

Like: dragging my feet through the year's dead leaves, rotting already and turning to slime.

Like: swinging my school bag around me in a circle, just in case it hit any ghosts.

Like: thinking.

Our road is quiet enough. In daylight you can see the old oak trees lining the sides and the scattering of holly beneath. There are walls made from rocks piled up high, with earth in between. I know that, because my brother helped repair them once to keep stock in. Really, the wall is just a heap of old sod and stone, but things creep and grow to hold everything together. When my brother pulled the roots out, a whole section fell down.

'Just look at that, Kate,' he said.

I asked him to name the ivy, saxifrage and bindweed that lay pulled around his feet. He did it for me, but I could see it bothered him that something that looked so strong could tumble so quickly.

Maybe I should have stayed on the bus. I could have got off at our gate and walked up to the house. I could have opened the blue painted door and gone in, but it was all too fast. Instead,

I'd escaped from Jimmy John popping bubble gum in my ear and Fat Wallace saying: 'Leave her alone, because of the day that's in it.'

And I wanted to walk. Even though I hate the dark and foxes can see in it much better than I can.

There's a sheltered place just ahead, back under the split-trunk tree. It's where the goat died. A big white Billy, with horns that tipped out and back to a point at each end. He had curls in between. Deceptive that! It made you think of little lambs and kiss curls, some sweet kind of innocence. Until you looked in his eyes. They were hard little slits that said: 'If you don't like what I am, then that's tough.'

My ma said it was because he'd hit into the breeding season and there just wasn't anything around for him to breed with. I don't know about that, but she knows most things.

That white Billy wasn't really white. Close up, he was yellow. He had a stink that could place him at a hundred yards. I didn't mind him much. At least I knew when he was coming close and I could hop onto the wall, or up a tree, until he passed by. He took on my ma though. She chased him back up the road, with a broom waving and her striped pinny flapping. You'd have thought she was a lion tamer, or something. She said she was just defending her own. She didn't want to see her vegetables shredded and her roses nipped. She broke the broom across his back and beat him over the head with the bristle end, but he didn't back down. He kept rearing up on two back legs and dropping those horns down towards her, over and over. My da had to come and catch him. There's a lot of leverage on horns that big. My da caught hold and forced them down to the ground. That Billy just had to submit.

They tied him to the tree with a bit of washing line, looping a strong knot so he didn't choke, and that's where he was shot. Three bullets. Or four if you count the one that missed. My ma had to bath and wash her clothes and my da had to burn his. The stink just wouldn't come out.

I forgot how fast the night comes in when the days are short. To my right is the hay field. In the summer, it bristles with crackling grass. One time I whirled around in a circle and plopped down in the centre, hidden, except for the telltale track. I know I shouldn't have flattened the long spikes, but I loved lying silent on my back, watching the clouds slip and slide gently over green fortress walls.

My brother followed the stepping track where I'd bent the stalks down. He lifted his feet and placed each one where my foot had fallen. His shoes were bigger, so he blotted out my steps, but he found me all the same. He came upon me so silently, and I was so lost in cloud dreams, that I didn't know he was there until he jumped and landed on me, holding my wrists to the ground and laughing with a wide mouth.

We rolled and rolled, flattening more grass, blotting out the sound of the mowing machine.

My da pulled us apart, roaring and spitting in his anger.

'What are you doing?' he demanded. 'Didn't you hear the mower? You could have been cut to pieces!' He struck my brother across the face.

'Don't ever try anything with Kate,' he said.

'You know I'd never do that,' my brother answered and he stared straight into my da's eyes, until he looked away and started kicking the grass.

This next oak tree is a friend of mine. I think it's safe to stop here for a moment and try to make my breath calm down. I think the tree will protect me from any harm. It has a fork low to the ground, so it's easy to jump up onto a scaly limb. You can walk along the branch, until you are high enough to sit where no one will notice and the fields stretch out around you. It's the best place to have a conversation.

'I don't really mean "all",' my brother explained. 'When I wrote it, I was angry and I didn't think how the words could hurt. Poor Kate.' He hugged me close and promised to scratch the 'all' from his words of hate. But I knew it wouldn't work. I was still part of the tally. In some way I didn't understand, I had failed him too.

There's a breeze picking up. I can hear it in the clicking twig fingers above my head. For a moment it sounds like a car in the distance, heading towards me, but it passes by in the darkness high above. I wonder if it blows ghosts along with it. Swirling up demons from other people's lives and whirling until they land somewhere else, maybe miles away, where no one knows what their moans and groans are all about. But that can't be right: the wind always whips quickly down our valley and there are still ghosts here. It isn't as easy as that to blow them away.

Everything is connected.

Like: Jimmy John saying to Fat Wallace: 'Don't touch her. You might catch something. And your dick will fall off.'

Like: my da holding onto my brother's arm and hitting him hard around the head as they whirled and whirled in the farmyard.

Like: my mother clutching a magazine to her chest and screaming to stop. Screaming that he can't help it. And when he'd left, she said to me: 'It's just like that old goat, Kate. There's none around here the same kind. He had to go. Better that, than a bullet through the head.'

Like: A magazine that I stole, because I half like it and I half don't understand it.

'This is an old backward place, Kate,' my brother said. 'People here would say "no" to anything that's new. They'd send the best opportunity marching off up the road, just because they don't want to face it. They're afraid that's all. They're afraid of me because I'm different. Don't think badly of me Kate.'

He kissed me gently on the cheek and wiped my tears with his finger. I begged him to stay, over and over. I twined my fingers in his hair and wouldn't let go, wanting to hold him forever. I refused to watch when he packed his bag. I shut my eyes when he walked down the road.

I wanted to say that I could never think anything against him. That he'd always been the best brother to me. That if he was different, then I wanted to be different too. If he hated this place, then so did I. I wanted to make a secret pact, but the words wouldn't fall out right, so I said nothing.

There's a taste in the air that's come in on the wind. It's not the tang by the ditch where a fox has marked his run. That only lasts a few paces and then it's gone. This is something cold and elusive, almost metallic. It breathes into the back of my throat and snags a memory. Maybe red at night does mean snow! I have a scarf in my bag, but that means stopping and lifting my arms from the straps. It means dropping the bag to the ground and hunting down among schoolbooks and leftover lunch. It might give time for the ghosts to catch up.

'There's no such thing!' my brother laughed. 'Here look.' He flung open the doors of the cupboard on the landing. There were towels, sheets and covers for the spare bed. He pulled out a white cloth and unfurled it like a cloud to drop over his head. We laughed, but it didn't change anything. I always knew that ghosts weren't like that. They live inside of you as much as in a cupboard or a bend on the road. They slip out as words from under my parents' door:

'He didn't get it from my side of the family.'

'What did we do wrong? We tried didn't we?'

'You shouldn't have hit him so hard is all I'm saying. That won't change anything. Did you see what he wrote on the side of the barn?'

'We were too soft. I should have thrashed it out of him years ago. If only I'd known, I could have done something. I'd thought him and Kate. You know. I'd thought they were always together, that something was going on. But I didn't want to see it, so I didn't look too close. Maybe if I had, I'd have seen the truth.'

'He was good to Kate. He always was. From the moment she was born he helped look after her. Did you see her crying when she saw what he'd written? He chased her halfway down the road, calling her back.'

Then there was just crying. Ma and Da. Their sobs slipping under the door like formless ghosts.

I can see a light now. It's shining out of the tall window in the gable end. It was by the window that my da stopped me. He looked at me sideways, as if he was trying to work something out.

'You don't need to tell people why he left,' he said. 'Just say he's got a job. Gone away to where the money is. Maybe in a year or two there'll be a wife and child.'

'There won't be!' I said.

He looked at me, through sad eyes.

'And what would you know?' he said. 'Just don't say anything. That's the safest thing.'

So I haven't.

There was no one to talk to anyway. No one to ask what everything meant.

I used to be afraid of our gate by night. I once saw an old crow fly up into the black sky. It made that noise that makes you think it's mocking, or knows something you don't. Black and ragged. It faded into the sky too fast. My da said that crows don't do that. That they don't like the dark any more than I do. He said I was just imagining things. Same as I always do.

My brother said that maybe that old tatty bird just wanted to say hello. That it was prepared to wait around and act a little different, just because it liked me and it wanted to; that eventually it just got too dark and it had to head off. I never found out which one of them was right, but I still look out just in case, as I lift the latch and step through.

There are no birds tonight, but there will be plenty of black and faded suits: people turned out too late to say 'hello'.

The grey, stone farmhouse is surrounded by cars. My bedroom is to the far right, with a half-window set back in the roof. My brother's room was right next door, so we could tap messages through the wall. I always forgot to knock when I opened his door. That's how I knew. A long time before the rest, I knew. But I never told anyone.

Behind the bright windows, my ma and da are moving slowly, polishing glasses and setting them down on the table. Pouring whiskey and sherry, slicing fruitcake. I don't even know if they've missed me yet. Maybe they didn't hear the school bus pass by or wonder why I hadn't come in with a bang of the door, sliding my school bag across the floor until it hit up against the range.

There are people talking behind the window: neighbours from up and down. I'm tired of being the only one who can't say anything.

Something wet falls on my face. The first soft flakes are tumbling. I stick out my tongue and only close my mouth when I have the act of communion completed.

The warmth of the kitchen is thick around me as I open the door.

'Ah Kate, I'm sorry now,' people start to say. They reach for my hands.

I shrug them off.

'He died of AIDS,' I shout. 'Do you know what that is? My brother was GAY!'

The hands reach out again. 'We know Kate. It's all right, Kate,' they say.

'Someone get her a small drop of whiskey, to calm her down.'

'My cousin's brother-in-law was the same way.'

'Sit down, sit down.'

'It's the big city life, that's all.'

'No one blames him, Kate. He was always that way.'

And my ma: 'You know! Oh my sweet Kate, you know!'

The kitchen lino slides. I tumble down one, two, three.

One: It was everyone's secret, not mine alone.

Two: Why did nobody say?

Three: Because they were protecting me.

And maybe four: That's why he had to leave.

The coffin is laid out in the back room. It's open because Mrs P from up the road says you don't catch it by sneezing, or looking, or touching a face. There are flowers all around, but I've brought a pocket full of green leaves: a posy full of saxifrage and ivy. I lay my leaves down around his shrunken cheeks. I hold his hand. It's cold and dead, heavy like a lump of clay from a fresh-ploughed field.

I sit for so long that my ma comes in and blows out the candles that are lit at my brother's head and feet. She puts her arms around me and I feel her muscles squeeze.

'Maybe it's not as dark as you think,' she says. 'You can see all sorts of things if you look hard enough.'

I can't though. I can't see how this lifeless thing is my brother. I can't see why he had to come home in a coffin, while we all sang 'ring a rosy' and pretended there was no such thing as the plague. I can't see how being left in the dark helps anything.

'It's the roots that hold everything together,' I say. 'When you pull those out, we all fall down.'

'We did what we thought was best,' my ma says.

It's snowing hard outside and the wind is picking and blowing a little stronger. It hurls the flakes against ditches and makes rolling waves over the flat fields. I can see by its brightness. There's a drift against the barn wall, covering the words in a layer of pure white.

We'll bury my brother tomorrow, down beneath the earth that grows grass to feed cows and ivy to twine walls, but can't sustain a rare bloom. For this one night, everything is open, raw and revealed. The truth is possible for a brief moment in time. In a day or two it will be covered back over again. Mrs P won't use her round mouth to repeat the word AIDS. My ma won't hold me tight and tell me that I'm not gay just because my brother was. This place will shut its eyes once more against something different walking along the roads and there won't be anyone for me to ask why a magazine full of naked men is an evil thing. But I won't pretend and I won't forget.

Some ghosts walk step by step at your side, whether you can see them or not.

Changes of Light

How can I describe this valley?

'A hard place,' my father said, when he first saw it. 'A place of grief, where scratching a living could never be easy.'

I didn't see that. I saw the beauty of hillsides covered in tumbled rock. I saw waterfalls pounding off the mountain after a long night's rain. I saw the small ruined houses and wondered who had lived there. I imagined children going in and out beneath the low stone lintels. I saw romantic, thatched roofs instead of open sky.

'Times have changed,' I said to my father. 'I just want to live here. I don't need to make a living from the land.'

I knew he was seeing small steep fields where a sheep could break a leg. I could see his gaze scouring for topsoil, trying to spot one small place where a hayfield might grow. Or a corner for a garden, where potatoes might have shelter from a strong south-westerly. He shook his head and shifted the tweed cap back a little. He didn't speak, but I knew he didn't approve.

When we got to the cottage it was no better. A small, damp place, surrounded by tall, black pines that blocked out the sunlight. My father half-closed his eyes, scanning the treetops and the roof of the house. I couldn't guess what he was really seeing.

I had loved the place as soon as I saw it. So much so that I'd tracked down the owner and walked the land over and over, trying to cut a bargain. When our prices had finally drawn together – each of us rushing, in our final moments of haste, to make a deal before either side backed out – then I had paused a moment. I didn't want to buy this place without talking to my father. I wanted him to put his feet upon this ground and say: 'Yes, it's fine to return to your roots. Yes, it's good to go back to a simpler life.'

The day was dull and low mist hung on the mountain when I brought my father to this house. The top of the pine trees shook with gusts of wind and a loose branch groaned. I had been charmed by the plate still on the table, by the seat with legs of different lengths – made to fit one place only on the uneven kitchen floor. I loved the slope down to the doorway, where years of tread had worn a dip in the threshold. The windows upstairs were low to the ground.

'Look,' I said. 'You have to kneel down to see out of them. They must have been made for children to peep out of.'

My father wasn't looking at the window. He stared up at the ceiling. The boards were painted white once, but now they were a mottled brown. There were gaps between them and small husks of grain dangled in cobwebs. A finger of light shone down onto his upturned face. It played among the grey sheen of morning stubble.

'The slates will be soft,' he said. 'And there are mice for sure, if not worse. How many years since grain was stored in the shed below? How many generations of mice have fed on the droppings from a sack of oats, or barley?'

'The cobwebs will soon brush away,' I said.

'It's what's behind the boards that I'd worry about.'

He bent forward, easing stiffly and balancing his weight with a hand on his knee. The low window gave a good view of a cracked concrete path. Two magpies hopped and sidestepped; so smartly dressed, they looked out of place among the nettles. He moved the cap again, forward and back.

'The windows weren't made for children,' my father said. 'It was impossible to raise the house up any higher. All the stones had to be lifted by hand. It's hard enough to lift a building stone to knee height. They were strong men in those days, but it wasn't the children they were thinking of when they built low houses and low windows.'

A wooden bed was still in the corner. A lake of candle-wax dribbled, frozen on the painted board at one end, with an inch of white household candle still at the centre. A jacket hung off a nail behind the door. One pocket was ripped and there was a piece of twine through a buttonhole. The nail was brown with rust and poked through a hole in the collar.

'There's no electric. Probably no water except a spring well – in the yard if you're lucky and much further afield if you're not.'

My father looked old in this house. The magpies tilted their heads. They hopped.

'Two for joy,' I said. One good clap of his hands and they would fly away.

We stood in the full depth of the chimney. There were seats to each side, but they were so ingrained with sticky blackness that neither of us chose to sit down.

'At least there's plenty of sky up there,' he said. 'But there'll be inches of tar and soot on the sides of the chimney. If you light a fire big enough to move the damp from the house, you'll probably set fire to it. Have you ever seen a fire in a chimney like this? I've seen flames roaring out of the top; scattering sparks all around. The whole end of the house had a crack from top to bottom with the heat. The fire only stops when there's nothing left to consume. It's no use pushing a brush up something like this. You would have to drag a holly bush up and down on a piece of rope.'

He was telling me that life hadn't been easy, how he could read the story of this place much better than I could. I sat down at the table.

'What do you think, Daddy?' I asked. 'Should I buy it? They know I'm interested. They're pushing to close the deal, but I wanted you to see it first. I hoped you would want to live here with me.'

My father put his hand up to his cap. He moved it forward and back, forward and back, then he removed it altogether and ran a hand across the exposed skin on top.

'Three generations,' he said. 'That's all it takes. You want to step back into your grandmother's shoes. Do you see the one plate? Do you see the burn marks all along one edge of the table, from too many lonely cigarettes? Do you smell the damp turf that still lies in the ashes of the fire? That's what's soaked into this place: hard work and loneliness.'

Outside, the sun had broken through and there was light playing in the top of the pines. On an impulse I slipped my hand into my father's fist, prising open the clenched fingers until they relaxed and held themselves loosely around my own. There was warmth in his grip and something familiar to the size of his hand wrapped around mine. My father dipped his head as we went through the doorway and the magpies flew high into the trees. There was another one now.

'Three for a girl,' I said. 'That must be me.'

We walked round the side of the house. There were low stone walls and steep narrow steps that led on and up to a grassy bank. The sun struck here and warmed the green of the rocks that looped round in a curve.

'Look,' I said, kneeling down on the ground and parting

the grass. 'Do you see? There must have been a garden here.'

There were the first purple and yellow tips of crocuses about to emerge. I pulled him across the sunlight and shadows.

'There's a rambling rose at this end of the house.' I said. 'Do you see the green leaves just starting to uncurl? It must be beautiful when the flowers are open. And here's the well, just a few feet away and close enough to the kitchen door. Do you see the mosaic set into the concrete, here by the step?'

'Old ware from the house,' he said, kneeling to touch, brushing aside the fallen leaves. 'A broken jug, is my guess, and here a piece of plate. We had the same pattern at home.'

'Someone made this, Daddy. Someone who lived that grim life, in that depressing house you talked about. Someone there had enough joy to make a garden and to gather pottery, to make this mosaic. Maybe some of that would soak into me too.'

'Maybe you're right,' he said. 'And maybe you're wrong.'

I puffed the air from my lungs in exasperation.

'Did you taste the water?' he asked, stepping up to the well. 'It could be brackish, or sour.' He put his hand down into the cool green of the ferns growing near the water's edge.

'Look at that,' he said, lifting a tin mug, then swooping it down into sunlight reflecting off clear water. 'Here's a cup set out for a thirsty stranger to take a drink.'

I watched him clean the dirt from the cup with a white

pocket-handkerchief, wondering who washed and ironed them for him now. My mother had put a fresh one there every day.

'It's the last one,' he said, reading my mind. 'Your mother hated it when we two argued. She said we were too much alike. Too stubborn.'

He polished the tin until it shone, then dipped the cup in the well, filling it to the brim. Drops dribbled on his chin as he drank. 'That's cold,' he said. 'Right from the heart of the mountain. With water like that, a lot would be possible.'

Steps at the end of the house led up to a door. They were dotted with navelwort in the cracks, and pools of water had gathered in the backward tilt. We climbed and stood on the top step, to capture a new view back down the valley. In the distance, smoke curled up slowly from a whitened chimney.

'Maybe I could live here and be inspired by whoever made the carefully curving walls, whoever set the stone steps, so they wouldn't be too large a stride and they wouldn't tilt over,' I said. 'Maybe I could pick summer roses and look at the heather on the mountain and only admire the display of purple shades. Nobody would force you to live here too.'

'Let's not argue,' he said, pulling his hand from mine. 'I agree, those steps are well set,' he added with a smile.

The magpies landed with a harsh chatter. Were there seven now, or did I count one twice? We walked through a gap in the wall, where round stones had tumbled down. The sun was brighter now. It shone down in rays through the clouds. It looked like a painting of God's hand casting light upon the earth. I loved the drama of it all.

'Do you see the trees over there, all round in a ring? Do you see the way the light falls on them as if it were a stage? Do you see the way the ground slopes up?' my father asked. He pointed to a place set back from the house, no more than twenty metres away. I had hoped that he would notice. It was one of the things I loved about this place.

'It's a fairy fort. I'd bet good money on it. You'd maybe not like that so near to your door,' he said.

I had thought it would make a good garden, but I didn't say so. My father is a Christian man, but sometimes he can surprise me.

'Really? Well, it could bring luck,' I said hopefully. 'If we treated it right. With respect for the past.'

'Well that's possible too,' he admitted. 'It might not be such a terrible thing. The inhabitants might look on us kindly.'

I didn't know if he was teasing me. I'd never heard him talk this way before. He moved the cap again, tipping it to a jaunty angle on his head.

We walked the small fields and watched the speeding river that marked the western boundary. I wanted my father to see what I saw. I wanted him to fall in love with the high clouds and the sweet taste of pure air as it entered his lungs.

'There will be commonage up on the mountain,' he said. 'It would be best to fence it, but you'd have to fight over that. No one will want to let go of an inch of land. You'd have to make sure of the boundaries from the start. A feud is a serious matter in this sort of place.'

'There's no feud,' I laughed. 'Just you and me, some acres of mountain and a house that calls out to be a home again. I wouldn't care if my boundaries were crooked, or if someone else got a corner of my land, as long as they didn't take the river.'

'Well there you are. It starts with a river. And before you know it, you're pulled back into the old ways. There might be a bit of good turf bog that's cut off. Would you care about that?'

I caught the twinkle in his eye again and knew that he was trying to get a rise out of me.

'What about the fairy fort?' I asked. 'Will we take a look at that?'

There was a circle of trees, all right, and a small stream running through at one side. The rise was slight and a bridge of rock and grass sod spanned the water. I couldn't see what made it into a fairy place. It looked too green and damp. And didn't forts have high walls?

'Ah, but you'd know,' he said, when I asked.

The magpies were above us in the trees. I couldn't count their number, but their chatter was loud and harsh in my ears.

I had to raise my voice, so that he could hear: 'The birds seem to like it.'

The hand of God threw rays of light around the trees. They scattered and spattered and for a moment I was dazzled. From the corner of my eye I thought I saw a movement. But then it was gone.

'I miss your mother.' The words burst from him.

A tingle prickled up my spine. My father wasn't a man to talk about his feelings. He hadn't shed a tear that I had seen, since my mother died. The movement was there again, but he didn't seem to notice. It was just the play of light across a special place. It was just imagination tickling around my brain.

He took the cap from his head and looked inside, as if seeing for the first time, what the label might tell him. He ran his finger round the band and loosened it with a practiced thumb.

'She always wanted to come back,' he said at last. 'It was the one thing that ever came between us, in all our time. Your mother wanted to come home, to look for a small place to retire to, in her own land, among her own people. She just wanted to be where her heart sang to the air and the memories that were all around her. She never got the chance.'

'I didn't know!'

I put my hand on his collar. It was thick and warm, with no rust to mark it.

'Let's make a home here,' I said. 'We'll rebuild the house. We'll dig the flower bed and plant more roses. It's not too late.'

I waved my hand to scatter those foolish black and white birds. I took his hand in mine. My fingers curled around his: reversing roles, offering comfort, offering protection. My hand would never be big enough to wrap the whole way round, but I would do the best I could.

I led him from the fairy fort and back towards the yard. I didn't want his words to be coloured by the hand of God. I didn't want his decision to be forced by a trick of light.

I looked at the sheen of gold, as gorse began to break open its buds. I looked at the high sky, as the layers of cloud moved in two directions at once. There was a hawk hovering high on the mountain. My father watched its perfect balanced stillness, waiting to plunge one way or another. Light flickered through the pines. It played across the flaking plaster at the front of the house; catching the raindrops in a cobweb that stretched from gutter to window ledge; making a mirror image of the tall, dark trees in the window glass. The magpies had all gone. The house was silent, waiting. The hawk broke through the layers of air currents. It had seen something that I could not and plummeted at last, sure upon its course.

'We could cut those trees to get a better view,' my father said.

'You can't eat a view,' I laughed, but I knew then that everything would be all right.

'Is that really a fairy fort?' I asked as we drove down to the house with the white chimney, to shake a hand over whiskey and a deal done.

My father laughed. 'Probably not,' he said. 'Just a haggard. A place to round livestock into. Or a place to store haystacks and turf for the winter.'

'Ah.'

'Did you want fairies?' he asked. 'They can be hard to live with. Not just pastel wings and granting wishes. The small people can play tricks too, or take offence as easy as that.' He snapped his fingers in the air. 'They can change your life as easily as the light changes on the mountain.'

We both knew that he was joking.

How can I describe this valley? Rocks that can't be eaten. Water that's as cold as ice. Moss green stones that ring a hidden garden. Birds that bring sorrow and joy.

A touch of magic that shines through in the changes of light.

BLOODLINES

There's an orange tree on the kitchen window ledge. It drips with fruit. Mother put it there to be admired.

'No point growing oranges,' she says 'if no one can see them.'

The blossom smells divine, but it makes me sneeze. The fruit is perfect, but it can't be picked. I'm not permitted to discover if the juice is sharp or sweet. I don't have enough fingers and toes to count the times that I've bitten my tongue so I don't reply: 'No point growing oranges in a kitchen window. No point in blocking out all the light. No point at all if it's just for show. If we only see the polished skin and never find out what the fruit is like inside.'

Calluses can grow on a tongue if it's bitten enough. They may not be obvious, but the owner of the tongue can feel them. The same goes for a heart, or the blood that pumps through the veins – well, blood can't grow calluses, but I'm sure that the inside of a blood vessel can.

I am fifty years old. Almost! The orange tree isn't that old, although Mother throws up cloud covers and smokescreens if I ask.

She told me that more young people are living at home. They don't fly the nest, because they can't afford the sticks to build one of their own. They spend their money on the feathers instead – the finery – that's what Mother says. I wouldn't be so fast to condemn what anyone does. Here am I, after all, almost fifty years old! That's a fact that Mother doesn't mind repeating, although I'd prefer to bite it back. I'm still living at home because I always have. Some things don't change. The world might move outside the windows, but in our kitchen it's always the same: there's Mother, the orange tree and me.

'That sponge cake is a bit hard.'

'Dip it in your tea.'

'A lump's fallen off.'

'Use your spoon to fish it out.'

No one from the outside, looking in at the window and peering through the mass of shiny leaves, would understand why change is such an undesirable thing. Of course no one would actually look in, or hear what we said. Our kitchen is down in the basement and there are bars across the glass to prevent the outside from coming in.

'The leaves are dusty.'

Mother says the same thing every day. I catch up the dishcloth.

'Not that one. The other one. Foolish girl, you should know by now.'

There are lots of things I know. For example: the leaves of an orange tree don't need polishing every day; Mother has called me foolish more times than she has used my given name; and I like to use the wrong cloth just to bait her.

When the sun shines in a certain way, it makes a shadow grow on the wall. It makes the shape of another tree in white and black. The spaces define the leaves, the stems and the dangling fruit. We like to watch the shadow and the flicker of light.

'One day, the orange tree will grow as big as that.' Mother nods her head to the wall and I nod my head in reply.

Sometimes I know she's wrong. If the tree grew that big, then it would spill out of the window and we'd have to break the bars to let it grow outside. Other times, I wonder. Mother always said I would live to grow big and she was right about that. In spite of everything, I've grown to fill the armchair; even though it's a bit of a squeeze and sometimes my waist has red marks where it's pressed against the fabric and rubbed in a line. Mother is like a little bird. She likes it when I tell her that. Maybe she imagines flying between branches of orange blossom in a clear blue sky.

'Will I make a fresh brew? Give me that cup, I'll give it a rinse.'

I can't bear the look on her face as she peers into the cup and tries to fish the cake crumbs out. I'd sooner boil the kettle again. The tea bag is still on the side of the sink.

'We should order more milk.'

I raise my voice in case she doesn't hear. There's little enough to eat in the fridge: just two ready meals in the freezer box, we should order more.

'Michael will call round later. I'll give him the list.' Mother lifts her hand as she speaks. She waves at the pencil and paper on the table.

'Do we have enough toilet roll?'

The kitchen is warm, but Mother feels the cold. I'd throw wide the window if it wasn't nailed shut. I'd let some fresh air blow through. The same air has been puffed in and out of our lungs for year upon year. It's hard to know how anything fresh could blow in at the door upstairs and drift down the basement steps. Sometimes I look out through the letter box. Mother does the same. We feed our slip of paper out to Michael and he brings back the things that we need. With the pension, we manage to make ends meet.

It wasn't always this way. I remember walks in the park. I held her hand tight and she circled mine like a glove. We walked twice round the duck pond and back by the swings. If I was good, and a bench was free, we would watch for a while. If I close my eyes, I can still picture fat, pale legs flying up in the air. And ankle socks.

We used to have a television in the kitchen, but Mother took it upstairs. I can hear it mumbling away in her bedroom and sometimes I catch a few words.

'We don't want you upset,' she said.

That was the end of that. Once the *upset* word was introduced, there was nothing to do but back down. I prefer reading, of course. *Wuthering Heights* is my favourite. Only in my version I picture Heathcliff, not Cathy, at the window. A confession now: sometimes I try to press my lips to the glass between the orange branches.

Mother was a 'looker' in her day. You can tell from the photographs. The album used to be green, but now it's worn through to black where a thumb has pressed, time upon time, against the edge. I half remember Grandmother. She died when I was young, but the disappointment in her eyes is fixed in a photograph. There's one of all of us: one, two, three. Down in a row all staring ahead. Not a smile, but a tilt of the eyes that says we were taught in the same school of 'how to stand for a photograph'. Grandmother is in black. She's mourning something. The passing of a husband perhaps, or the 'looker' of a daughter, who managed to produce a child without a husband to catch or to mourn: he passed too quickly to grab.

Even 'lookers' lose their looks when they are old. Mother has lines round her mouth where she puckers it up to sip. Even when she isn't drinking tea her lips stay like that. When I'm annoyed with her, with the things that she does, I think 'arse mouth' in my head. I learned that from the television, but I don't say it out loud. It's small recompense, this silent rebellion.

It's little enough to count against the years spent watching the mouth pucker up.

Almost fifty! Happy Birthday to me! I could sing to my-self tomorrow and eat the remains of a dried sponge cake. We might have new tea bags, to celebrate. And lasagne in a shiny silver tray that only has to be popped in the oven.

They sang Happy Birthday in school when I was six. The teacher made the class sing for each child on their special day. If the child was popular then it didn't sound too bad. For the ones that weren't liked, the song scattered to different speeds as some children rushed through and other ones dragged. My birthday song was a neat clip. The children sat up and made an effort to concentrate. They reached the end at the same moment, even though some sang in high voices and others forgot the words. I wasn't popular. No never that. But I was the biggest and strongest child in the class.

'What are you daydreaming about?' Mother asks.

I stand with her teacup in one hand. The other hand sends the spoon around. Around and around.

'It's the third time for this bag,' I answer her back. 'It needs a good stir to get any colour out.'

'We need more sugar.' Her spoon grates against the stuck grains in the bottom of the bowl.

I look at the list: 1 carton milk, 1 bag sugar.

'I want lasagne!'

'Ah but there's no point,' Mother says back.

I know she has her plan. I know that when she chooses her moment, she expects me to do what she asks. She thinks I'm no different than when I was a child. She says that people don't change, not really, not right inside. She says that she still thinks she's twenty-three and as pretty as a picture, until she looks in the mirror and remembers otherwise. Her picture of me has been framed in her mind, as if it were no more than a faded photograph: legs akimbo, eyes cast down, tears dripping down to the ground and my mouth open to say how sorry I am, how I love her, how I want to stay with her always.

Mother has cancer. Cancer. Cancer. It's not so hard to say with a bit of practice, but she doesn't like to name it, so the word rolls in my mouth and doesn't tumble out until I'm alone in my bed.

It started as a lump in her breast. I found that hard to understand. Her breasts are so small that they are barely lumps themselves. Nonetheless the cancer started there: cancer or Cancer or CaNcEr, it's all the same word, with the same implication, however it's spelled out. She put a finger on the lump one day, is what she said. There was red in her cheeks when she spoke. If the image of a finger touching her breasts was going through her mind, it was also going through mine. She suggested we look it up: to take our minds off the thought of where else her finger might wander, was my guess. We took the medical encyclopedia down off the shelf. It's an old book, but: 'A lump is a lump; and the C word doesn't change with new ideas,' was what Mother said. She was determined she could beat it without any help, but she added paracetamol onto Michael's list a few months back and a large pack arrives every week.

The pain moved to her side and her back. She said it was the same pain that her own mother had. When I opened my mouth to find out more, she waved a finger and shook her head so I knew not to ask.

I care for my mother. She finds that hard. For so long she cared for me, then the tables turned. Or maybe care is too grand a word! I do as I'm told. I made that agreement long ago, when I thought it meant sitting still if needed or keeping my mouth shut while adults talked.

If I was making a list with my mother's pencil, if I were listing my jobs, I would write: lifting her in and out of bed; lifting her in and out of the chair; lifting her on and off the commode; wiping her bum; wiping the leaves of a plant. Of course I make tea and more than this, but most days go round and round repeating small tasks.

I stare into the mirror above the sink and fire silent questions at the reflection: lank, long hair tied back, bitten lips, dark marks beneath my eyes. I don't answer back. I stick my tongue out.

This is what I ask, when my reflection raises an eyebrow: do you want to know why we spend our days in the basement? Why we don't go out, and only give and receive through a letter box? Do you want to know why Mother hides our lives behind an orange tree? She fears her own death, but do you want to know why she fears life more than that?

I get out another tea bag. A fresh one. There's no point in being stingy on the ante-birthday: the day before the big event.

'Do you want another cup?'

Mother doesn't hear. She's fallen asleep in her chair. I give the bag an extra squeeze, to darken the brew while she can't complain.

When I was young, I went to school. Some things get tangled, but I don't think I was bad. I don't think that I did too much harm until the day of the big *upset*. I hurt a child. I thought she was a friend.

'She hurt me first,' I protested, but her hurt could be seen on the side of her face and mine was locked inside. There's a type of pencil sharpener where a screw comes out. The blade is tiny, but quite sharp. If you rub the metal against a stone it gets sharper still.

'You're lucky,' Mother reminds me as often as she can. 'You could have been locked up in prison for what you did. You're lucky that I hid you here. That I keep you safe.'

I like this room really. I sleep near the stove. I piss in the sink and Mother used to empty the chamber pot when I did the other thing. I didn't mind at night if she locked me in. I never felt *upset* in the same way again, but Mother said that it was best not to risk anything. A teacher called once to the door. I heard Mother's voice. She sounded sad: 'I had to send her away to stay with my sister. She couldn't go back into school after what she did.'

That was that.

Michael, our neighbour, has known Mother for years. She likes him. He used to call and chat in the doorway. If I pressed my ear to the basement door, I'd hear her voice go soft and she'd giggle like he'd said something funny. That was always the way that she talked to him; until she decided one day that she had 'lost her looks' and would only speak to him through the letter box.

'I might have got married,' she said one time. I rubbed at shiny leaves with a cloth and bit my tongue. 'If it wasn't for you. Now I'm too old and you are too. If I could wind back the clock I'd let them put you in prison. I wouldn't hide you a second time around.' That was when a pain shot through her side. She doubled over and gasped for breath. I took a long time to find the paracetamol. She'd stopped opening the door to Michael by then.

He still calls every day for a list and brings back the shopping. I have to carry Mother up from the kitchen. She sits on a chair by the letter box. She talks through the wood of the door, through the paint. I look around and I think. This house is big. It stacks up high with rooms on top of each other in a pile. Mother keeps keys in her pocket. She opens the door so I can lift the bag from the doorstep, once Michael has left. The air and light hits my face like a rush of wings. Before I can get *upset*, I push the door shut and Mother turns the key again. When we go back down to the basement, she locks us both back in.

She's so frail that when I do that other thing in the chamber pot – the shit or shite, but I can't use the words in front of her – I have to go upstairs to empty it out myself. Mother is afraid of that, but what can she do? I run up and down the stairs, counting rooms, counting steps, counting windows, and looking out of some. I flush that thing away down the toilet. I pull the chain. Then I go back to Mother. She doesn't sleep while she waits. Her mouth puckers round when I come back down. She throws me the key and I lock us back in.

'We can't go on like this,' has become her new refrain.

So there's the plan. Only one more time to get *upset* then the pain will be gone. She has it all prepared.

There are no sharp knives in the kitchen. 'We don't need them,' Mother says. There are spoons for eating pasta bakes and cereals. There are spoons for stirring tea. I once tried to push a fork through my hand, so if I only have a spoon now, then I've only myself to blame. No edges, no blades, no sharpeners for pencils, although the one for Mother's list is always pointed and well maintained.

The birthday is almost upon us. We stay up late. If the hands turn round to midnight before I carry her upstairs, then the night is shorter, Mother says. She usually tells me to lock myself in, to hide the key and to forget it again. The basement is where I live: where I have to live until the end of my days. But she's decided that this is the moment for change.

'Good girl. Don't forget. Just give me a few moments. I'll be waiting.' Mother pats my hand as she speaks. I tuck her in.

There's a knife on the kitchen table. It has a sharp point. It was part of the list for Michael on the day before and he never questions what we need. I move aside my plate and use the point to write in the wood: FIFTY. Now I am! The clock is ticking one hour off my birthday and after that it will tick another one. Mother has set me a task.

'We can't go on as we are. It's not fair to either of us. I should have ended this years ago, but now I'm in pain and will die anyway, and you, well you just have to be strong.'

I lay the blade across my wrist. It's cold. One small push and there will be blood. I remember it still from when I was six: a drip, a pool, and a line of red across my hand. Just one small push across her neck and after that my wrists: that's all that Mother wants.

The clock ticks down the minutes as my birthday keeps its steady march along. If I count with the seconds and act at ten, I'll do it! I will! One, two, three …

… at ten, I pluck an orange from the tree. It leaves a broken stem behind. It fills my palm. I place it on the table top. The knife is light. The point tilts down. I press. The cut is swift and neat, so two halves fall apart. They ooze. Each segment is a bloody one. The ragged grooves of FIFTY fill with juice. I dip a finger in and taste. I need to know if a blood orange tastes the same as an ordinary one.

I made a promise once: 'I won't be bad again. I won't. I promise. No matter how *upset* I get, I won't be bad.'

Legs akimbo, eyes turned down, tears dropping on the ground, I lift my arms. Pale wrists move, unmarked, before my eyes. In a room above my head, Mother stretches her neck on a feather pillow.

I can tick down the list: her pulse, my wrists and oranges. The bloodlines run. I am fifty years old. Happy Birthday to Me! If I don't do it now, I never will.

At first I try the wrong key, but the next one turns. Wind hits my face as I rush outside to the air and the dark. I fly beyond the window-bars, where a hedge runs wild. Where branches throw their shapes upon the ground. I curl like a ball and close my eyes. Until Michael stops his footsteps on the path. Until he hunts me out. Until he helps me up and brushes me down and uses his long, patient fingers to unravel the knots in my hair, in my mind, in my life.

Later. Maybe much later, Michael tells me that Mother died in the night. Something burst inside. He says that I am the last of a damaged line. He'll keep me safe. He kisses my bitten lips. He'll help me hide …

High Nellie
and the Far Horizon

My mother was in the late stages of labour when she cycled to get the midwife. Everyone said she was stone mad: she'd had three children already and should have known better. For the first two years of life I had no hair at the sides of my head, just a thick black tuft across the top. It was the mark of the saddle my daddy said. He always got a laugh out of the story and people never asked why Mother had needed to make that ride instead of him.

As I got older I understood about Daddy.

It was Dreadlock Dan who suggested I should write down the story of my life.

'You're so old, May,' he said, 'and you must have seen so many amazing things.'

Tact isn't a strong point with Dan. In truth, I'm not exactly sure how old I am and there's no one left who would remember. He set me thinking though.

'Your Daddy's a great man for the drink.'

I heard this so often that I truly did think he was great. There was no one who could down a pint as quickly, or dance so wildly after an evening with a whiskey bottle. It took many years before I noticed the lines around Mother's eyes and the way her lips puckered in distaste. My sister had to spell the truth out to me. She whispered it behind the turf shed, her voice full of disapproval for my needing to be told. Perhaps I felt guilty. In any case, my brothers and sisters left home while I was still growing. It was an unspoken agreement that I would be the one to stay.

I love my home on the western side of the mountain. It is a low house hidden beneath a coat of whitewash. Winter storms do their best to beat the greyness back into its fabric. As years go by, both the house and myself more closely resemble the rocks all around.

Dan says the house is worth a fortune. He says that some wealthy German would pay hundreds of thousands for the view alone.

I tell him it isn't just a view. I tell him it's a reminder of all that's gone before. At this point he says 'Wow' or 'Amazing' and exchanges a look with one of the friends he has brought to visit. His friends have names like Izzy or Mash and they think nothing of filling my black kettle from the spring well and swinging it over the fire without asking.

'Tell us about High Nellie, May,' Dan says with a smile. He pushes one side of his long matted hair back behind an ear. Even at my age I can tell he's charming. I never know if one of the women he brings is a wife. I never know if the scattering of children with names like Feather and Flake are his own. He's talked of recording what I say, of writing my story down himself.

'Everyone can write,' he says. 'They just need a good tale to tell.'

'What's so good about a woman that's never been more than twenty miles from the place that she was born?' I ask.

'But that in itself is amazing. You've lived through inventions like cars, aeroplanes and computers and it's just amazing that you've seen all that from here.'

I wonder at his ability to be amazed. I wonder at his speech. I wonder at the flat English vowels.

'High Nellie?' he says as a gentle reminder. 'The bike?' he adds with another look towards his friends.

I know that he wants my bike. I know that he has told his friends all about it. I know that he is 'amazed' by the high black handlebars, the sit-up seat and the basket in front. I know he thinks that a woman of my age can have no use for a bike. But I have plans for Nellie.

The bike that my mother used was old and rusty. The chain locked solid through inactivity in the year following my birth. The front wheel developed a severe and mysterious twist and was never replaced. Any travelling we needed to do, in the first years of my life, was by donkey and cart. Daddy sat on the front edge of the cart and we piled behind, or ran beside the iron-shod wheels if the weight was too much.

The donkey was a stubborn thing. It ambled on the outward journey, looking worn down and old. It stopped to graze when it wanted and trotted wildly in a lopsided gallop if it felt the urge. Return journeys were always fast. The donkey remembered a twist of hay waiting at home. It was a lucky thing that the beast knew its own way back. Daddy wasn't much of a driver after a few hours in town.

No one uses a donkey cart now, except for getting money from tourists. I don't regret their passing. They were an uncomfortable and unpredictable way of getting around.

I can't help thinking about Dan and his talk of change. It's true of course. My nieces and nephews only visit because they can travel in aeroplanes and rush around in cars. They try to explain about computers and phones with no wires, but it doesn't matter a bit to me. They shiver by my little fire of turf and sticks. They beg me to close the door to keep in some warmth. They talk about electric radiators and showers. Of course they are very good to remember me.

Dan once asked me what I thought was the most important invention of the last century. He laughed when I said, 'My bicycle.'

I wanted to tell him that I knew it wasn't invented then. What I had meant was that it was the most important invention for me, and that I have lived for nearly a century. I was annoyed by his laughter. I didn't tell him my bike story. I was afraid he would tape it and try to write it down himself.

I was twelve years old when I got the bike. In fact it was about a week after my birthday: Mother had given me a bag of round toffees and a new dress. She cried a little as she baked a sweet cake for tea and I put my arms around her waist to comfort her. Tears plopped into the flour mix and I held her tighter, wanting to squeeze shut the place that was hurting her so much. I was twelve years and one week old, and I felt helpless as I watched Mother cry. She splashed her face with cold water and tried to smile. I asked what was wrong as she patted the cake into a round and slid it onto a tray. Currants poked through the mound of dough.

Daddy walked in the door. He had a big smile on his face and he smelled of strong spirits. 'What are you crying for, woman?' he said.

'You know well enough,' she answered.

'Well, you don't know as much as you think,' he said and catching her wrist, he pulled her out of the door. She held both floury hands awkwardly before her and nearly tripped on the worn dip in the threshold.

Leaning against the outside wall was a bicycle. It was black and shiny with a big basket in front.

'It's a High Nellie,' Daddy said.

Mother sobbed more loudly and grabbed Daddy by the shoulders. She gave him a big kiss on the mouth and a hug to go with it. For that evening, Daddy really was a great man.

Mother told me later that my sister had sent money from America to buy me a bike. Daddy had put the notes in his pocket and headed into town. My mother believed he would drink the lot.

Daddy told me later that he had got a great deal on the bike and had enough money left over to celebrate the bargain.

Dan brought me a present of some tomatoes from his garden. They were very small. I nearly told him to leave them grow bigger next time, but he's proud of his garden so I kept quiet.

He insisted that I visit his home and brought Fizz, or Wizz, along to hold one arm, while Dan held the other. I'd heard talk of course. People like something strange to discuss. Mostly the talk was about the dirt and the funny-shaped little houses.

They asked if I was worried living alone on the mountain, with all those hippies so close by. I don't feel afraid. Dan has been good to me.

He sat me on a chair outside his round tent of plastic and sticks. He made me a cup of tea. The women are friendly and one brought me a jar of jam. One of the children asked if I was a grandma. When I said that I'd never married, that I had no children or grandchildren of my own, she said I could be her grandma if I liked. Her hair was as tangled as a winter fleece, but she stayed still beneath my hand as I stroked it.

'Will you read me a story?' she asked.

'Of course,' I said, 'if the letters are big enough to see.'

Dan looked on in surprise as I read about a wind-up teddy bear that played a drum.

'You didn't think I could read,' I said and he blushed behind his hair. 'Mother made sure that I could.'

It didn't take me long to learn to ride a bike. I wobbled a bit for a while, but there weren't any cars on our road at that time. Mother held the saddle until I got balanced and then she let go. Nothing will ever beat the first downhill journey, the flying feel of the wind across my body, the whip of hair behind my head. I loved to cycle. I rode to the four crossroads and sat to watch the people go by.

Over the years, I cycled most places that could be gone to in a day and still got home for tea. I never travelled more than twenty miles, but I found the places where the best black-berries grew. I saw the tourists come into the hotel in town. I bought shoes at the fair and rode home, watching them shine round on the pedals. I got books when I could, wrapped up in a bag.

The basket held a packet of sandwiches and a bottle of tea. It held a young terrier for a few years, until she got too old and bad-tempered to enjoy a bike ride. I was cautious and always took a coat in case it rained.

Mother showed me how to clean and polish the wheels, how to pour oil in all the right places. I never left Nellie muddy or wet, and she always lived in a dry shed by night.

'This bike may have to last you a lifetime,' Mother said. 'You might never get another.'

I never needed another is the truth. I had some things fixed over the years and other things replaced, but Nellie was sturdy and strong. She never let me down.

I found Mother's hatpins in a drawer. They are fierce long things that it's hard to imagine poking so close to your flesh. They were old-fashioned even when I was young, but Mother never threw them away and nor will I. I remember looking at them when I was in my thirties. I suggested we use them to hold holly on a Christmas wreath. Mother laughed as she stabbed them into place.

'I was wearing these when I first met your Daddy,' she said. 'He wasn't always the way he is now.' The look in her eyes was so sad that I would have said anything to make her happy, but I couldn't think of any words.

'He always liked a drink, but not every day. Perhaps I should have seen it. I was too young to know better and I loved him.'

'It's all right,' I said. I truly meant it. I was happy with my life.

'No. It's not all right,' she said. 'I didn't want you to go the same way I did. I didn't let you meet men. I didn't want you to leave me.'

'I won't leave you. I've always known this is where I want to be.'

'You're a good girl, May,' Mother said and I didn't point out that my girl days were long gone.

I remember the hatpins because they were so sharp. I remember raised voices in the kitchen, while I was in bed: 'If you lay a hand on me, I'll stab you,' Mother shouted.

I flew down the stairs and saw my mother holding a long pin before Daddy's face. He was none too steady on his feet and I thought she might prick him by mistake. Daddy looked at me and crumpled his hat between his hands.

'I'll sleep in the barn,' he said and he shuffled off out the door.

That was the moment I knew I would never leave home.

Dan brought a new woman to visit. She's called Sheera. She had barely sat down to the tea when she started asking questions.

'Did you ever have any boyfriends?' she wanted to know.

I didn't mind really, but I knew others who would have. I didn't object to talking a little.

'No,' I said. 'There were no boyfriends. It wouldn't have been right you see. I always knew that I was staying at home. I knew that Daddy would need looking after.'

'Excuse me?' Sheera said. 'Do you mean you had to stay at home just to look after your parents?'

'It was the way things were done. It's different now. Young people leave the country all the time. They go to America and Australia. Well, they did in my day too, but one child always stayed home. I knew that it would be me.'

'So you stayed here and looked after your father?'

'And Mother too. They both lived long and healthy lives. The drink didn't take Daddy, although everyone said it would.'

'Let me get this straight,' Sheera went on. 'How old were you when your parents died?' She said this as if there was something shameful in a long and uneventful life.

'I was forty-eight, God rest them.'

I didn't say that I was a plain woman and that I'd never learned the ways of charming men. I didn't say I had stayed because Mother needed me.

I had one hard year: losing Mother, then Daddy within three months of one another. The neighbours helped. They knew everything there was to know about death and grieving. Some of them seemed to enjoy it.

I was forty-eight years old and alone in my world. I know that people made exceptions for me, but this didn't last forever. My one joy was Nellie. I rode to the crossroads and watched the cars. I sat on the grass bank, ate ham sandwiches and sipped tea from a bottle. I watched the strangers pass by and wondered what sort of lives they led. I wondered what they would make of my little house on the mountain, with its open door and its bright turf fire. I heard someone call me 'loose in the head'. It didn't bother me.

Age is an extraordinary thing. We go through years of trying to learn how to behave properly. 'Putting manners on you,' my mother said. We go through more years of believing we've worked everything out and know exactly what we are doing. As we hit middle age we begin to wonder, and in extreme old age we finally realise that no one cares and we can do exactly as we like.

Dan told me stories of campfires on foreign beaches. He told me of places where no one eats potatoes and the food is hot as fire. He told me about dancing with beautiful women and about playing the guitar until his arms were numb.

I told him about bringing home turf on the back of the donkey cart; about watching the swallows arrive each spring; about the pattern of rain on the mountain.

He came by with a woman called Flo and four children. They were polite and didn't ask private questions. The children ran around the yard, playing hide and seek. I could hear their shouts and their arguments. They came tumbling in the door asking if they could ride on the bike. One look at Dan and I knew he had put them up to it. I should put him out of his misery.

'The bike is called Nellie,' I said, 'and there is one last job she has to do for me yet. Until then, I don't want anybody else to ride her.'

I didn't say more, although perhaps these strange young people, with their different lives, would understand.

When Daddy died, I rode on my bike to get the doctor.

'Don't you mind the isolation?' he asked. 'You're very far out up here.'

'I like it,' I replied.

'You're free now,' he said gently. 'You could travel a bit. Visit your nephews and nieces. The world is a big place waiting to be seen.'

'No, thank you. I have everything I need here. I don't need to fly to find happiness.'

He looked at the stone floor, at the bright embers spilled around the hearth, at the table with its white cloth and a fresh baked loaf. I don't know if he understood.

Dan came alone. He looked at me shyly and scooped the dreadlocks back in both hands.

'What are you planning, May?' he asked. 'Why do you still need the bike?'

I really wanted to tell him. I wanted to explain about the freedom of flying down hills, about the sights that could be seen. I wanted to explain the adventure of travelling off in my thoughts with each car that drove by. I wanted to say that I had loved my mother and my daddy, even though she was just an ordinary woman and he wasn't a great man. I was happy with my life. I had always slept in the same house. I had always cooked at the same hearth. I had always known that things were no better, or worse, beyond the far horizon. But now I wondered if a woman who had never travelled more than twenty miles from home, could really be this sure. I saw the gentleness in Dan's eyes, but I still didn't tell him. I just wished him 'good luck and good bye', as he left through the door.

I visited a solicitor last week. I asked a neighbour to take me, but I wouldn't tell him why. I wanted to make sure that Dan gets the bike when I die. I didn't know his full name. 'Dreadlock Dan,' I said. 'Everyone will know who I mean.'

The solicitor wasn't happy. He wanted me to find out more details, but I made him write it down just as I said.

I only intended to sort out about the bike. I didn't want to think about anything else, but the solicitor kept pushing me. He wanted me to sort out the house and the land. I don't know if I did the right thing. I don't know if I was just annoyed by the lift of his lip when he talked about Dan. I bequeathed everything to the one person I know who thinks that my life is amazing.

Mother taught me about joy in small things. She loved the first hatch of chicks, the blue of a duck's egg, the soft sweetness of a fresh baked cake. She always buried her face in Daddy's new-washed shirt.

'We all have our place in life,' she told me. 'It's making that place sparkle that matters.'

'Do your days still sparkle?' I asked.

'I still love your daddy, if that's what you mean. I love the man that's not washed away by the drink. Love can make you do strange things,' she said. 'It never lets go, no matter what your age. It can make you stay in a place, or it can make you leave.'

'You didn't leave,' I said, 'and nor did I.'

'True love!' she laughed.

I pulled Nellie out of the shed last week and tried to sit on her. I couldn't even lift my leg above the pedal. I nearly fell over. I will have to accept that I am too old and it is too late to change the limits I have put upon my life.

I have abandoned my plan. I sat by my fire and cried.

When I was thirty, Daddy called me a heifer. He slapped my backside and said: 'A fine heifer like you should be sold at the mart.'

It was the one time I nearly left. I rode Nellie for hours until it got dark. But I couldn't keep going.

'He doesn't mean it,' Mother said, when I came home to my bed. 'In the morning he won't even remember his words.'

She was right of course. He kissed me on the cheek as I served his breakfast and called me his best girl.

When Dan called yesterday, I sat him down with a cup of strong tea.

'You can take Nellie,' I said. 'She's no use to me. I'm just too old.'

He tipped his head to one side. He put three spoons of sugar in his cup.

'Tell me what you wanted to do, May,' he said.

I had wanted to make one last journey. But I couldn't talk now about freedom, or about limits. I couldn't explain about wanting to take one look at the wider world, so that I could truly say I was happy with my small portion of it. I didn't even know how far I had hoped to go. I couldn't explain, but I asked one thing of Dan.

'Will you take Nellie for a spin?' I said. 'Take her more than twenty miles. At least one of us should get that far.'

Dan came today with Izzy, driving a big red van. He picked up Nellie and put her in the back. I thought he would just drive away. I wanted more time to say goodbye.

'Get your coat,' Dan laughed.

He helped me climb up into the seat at the front. He pulled the seat belt across me and clipped me in. We bounced down the mountain with the windows open and the wind blowing through. We drove faster than a bicycle, but we looked over fuchsia hedges and into green fields patterned with sheep.

'Watch the clock,' Dan said, pointing to a dial at the front.

I saw the number twenty, turn to twenty-one and then we stopped.

They helped me onto Nellie, one on each side, and held me firm while I pedalled along the road. I felt the familiar turn of the wheels, the push of my thigh.

If life had chosen that moment to escape from me, I would have been content. To enter the world with the mark of the saddle at one end and to leave it with the same mark at the other would have been just fine. But these are things we don't get to choose.

Dan left me outside my door.

'Was that what you had wanted?' he asked.

I nodded my head.

'You know something,' he said. 'My friends and I, we had to do a lot of travelling until we found this place. You were lucky enough to be born here. You never needed to travel to find what you already had.' He winked at me. 'It's amazing,' he said.

'I know that now,' I smiled. 'I always knew it really. I just wanted to take one peep beyond the far horizon.'

I waved as they drove away. I pushed my door wide open. I looked forward to a bright fire, a pot of tea and a cut of brown bread.

Comparable, Identical, One and the Same

He's snoring. Loud farting grumbles that make Lili's face hot and prickly. She wants to walk past. She wants to pretend that the shiny red car on the corner is really her dad's car, not the brown one that leaks, snorts and bubbles through the open window.

She hates brown. Nobody else has a car the colour of sludge. If you play the game of spotting cars and seeing who gets the most, people always choose red or silver, or maybe blue. No one but a shit would choose brown.

The door clicks, but not too loud. The seat prickles through to her legs. The snoring invades her right ear. She winds up the window to trap the noise inside the car.

Lili opens her school bag. She makes a list of cool and uncool on two sides of a page. Cool is easy:

> Silver, this year's cars
> Mr Gordon who teaches music every Tuesday
> Tight blue jeans
> Hair beads
> Sleepovers
> Thick mascara
> Sexy walks

She could go on forever.

Uncool is being picked up from school by her dad.
After that it isn't just uncool, it's revolting:

> Big belly
> Snoring
> Brown

Lili wants to be good at English. She wants to gather information. It's important that she looks closely. Then, when she is ready, she will be able to spill everything onto a page.

'Realism,' Miss Falvey says, 'is missing from your work.'

Bitch is a new word. A real word, born from observation.

Down around the corner, skip two three. In and out the alley-O and back to me.

Who invented chain-link fencing? It's supposed to stop things from flying out of the schoolyard. It doesn't though. Looks zip straight through: their smiles are broken into green, wired diamonds.

Most girls wear trainers. Some have black clonky shoes with fat heels. Lili knows about sets from maths. The clonkies are a set. The trainers are a much bigger set. The two don't overlap.

If you look closely, there are little sets inside the bigger ones. The Nikes and Cons are a subset. The Hi-Tec definitely don't belong there. The pointy shoes think they deserve a set of their own.

Do dirty laces go in a different set from clean ones?

Miss Falvey says that all men are created equal in the eyes of the Lord. She says it so many times that Lili wonders what she really means. In any case it's hard to picture her Lord's eyes. It's much easier to see Miriam Byrne's, or Eleanor Flick's.

Glasses aren't really a subset. They're mixed all through the other sets. You can have Nikes and gold rims, Hi-Tec and tiny rectangular frames. Even two of the clonkies need glasses to see the blackboard.

Dad stops snoring. In fact he stops breathing. There is a pause, a long and silent space. Lili could tap his hand as it lies, trout-like, on his trouser leg. She could insert a finger into his open mouth and touch his pink gums, his thick tongue. She could probe his tonsils and bring him back to life in a retching stream of puke. Or, she could just slide a bit further down in the seat.

The clonkies notice. Lili can tell by the angle of their shoulders. She can tell by the way they lean against the school wall, dissected into dainty green diamonds.

It's not so hard. She can wait. If only her eyes weren't pulled back and pulled back and pulled back to the other side of the fence.

Dad starts to breathe again. At least he isn't snoring now, only gulping air as if it was a good way to dry off the spit from his tongue.

Slip. Slap. Slip. Slap. Rope against the tarmac.

> Mr Brown is a very fat man
> He teaches his children all he can
> First of all he makes them dance
> Out of India and into France
> Out of France and into Spain
> Around the world, GO HOME AGAIN.

Eleanor Flick was born in London, but that doesn't count. Her parents are Irish and they'd only moved back; not moved to where they didn't belong. Eleanor Flick was *popular* and so was her song.

There was a competition for some toothpaste company one time. Each class had to smile at the camera. They chose the biggest smiles, the whitest teeth. Lili smiled until her cheeks hurt.

'A smile shows how happy you are inside,' Miss Falvey said.

That was probably why Lili didn't win.

The light goes off in the classroom. Miss Falvey will come out soon. Her long white legs will go pick, picking across the yard.

'Go home girls,' she shouts at the few remaining trainers and the group of clonkies. 'I've told you not to hang around the yard after school.'

She shoos like a mother hen rounding up chicks. If only she would give a peck with that long, white beak.

Tap. Tap. She knocks on the window. Dad snorts and opens his eyes. He rubs them with his brown trout hands.

'Mr Kapadia,' she says, 'I thought Lili had to go to the dentist an hour ago?'

He looks confused.

'My dad has to work nights. He's tired. It's not easy for him.' Lili winds up the window. She leaves a small gap. Just big enough for a few words to slip through.

'And you're wrong. You should look *equal* up in the dictionary!' Her hands tremble as she closes the gap. She knows she'll be in trouble tomorrow, but today there is a pane of glass between her and the rest of the world.

Miss Falvey shakes her head and pick, picks her high-heeled way to the shiny red car. She squeezes her hand and the lights flash as the door unlocks.

'I'm sorry,' Dad says. 'You should have woken me up.'

'It's all right,' Lili answers. 'It'll make no difference if we go today, tomorrow, or the day after that. Nothing will change. I'll open my mouth and the dentist will look inside. He'll see whatever there is to see.'

'Good girl.' Dad squeezes her hand.

The car starts smoothly with the turn of the key.

Precious Little

My feet are silent as a dung beetle. No! Better than that. They are like a snake that slithers to hide in the tin roof, looking for a cool place to sleep: but I think a snake would prefer the folds of banana thatch. Hard foot skin tips against the beaten mud and rolls from heel to toe as I sneak past. Mama sleeps on her mat. She doesn't stir. Even the slide of my dress over my back or the swish as I tie a rag around my hair doesn't make her smile and raise her head. If a snake did slip into the hut, if it swung down in a loop and stuck out a tongue to flick at her skin, if it stuck its poison in deep so the snake-bite-spit could do its work – even if! – Mama would look the same. For a while she'd be not-dead, but still with a flutter of breath like white moth wings.

She wasn't always that way. Sometimes the fever came on her and she'd lie and sweat. One day, two. Then she'd be back on her feet and swinging her hips. The sparkle in her eyes wasn't hidden by bigger-than-big-sack eyelids back then. Auntie told me to let Mama lie still, to give her water and nothing to eat. But I wouldn't trust what Auntie says. She has slit eyes that flick. She sees too many things, even though her sight has to travel from her hut to ours across the dirt in between. Sometimes I think she can look through the crinkles of tin and see the two hens that Mama keeps hidden in a box at the back of the hut. Her eyes watch me pluck green grass, green leaves. Her nose can sniff out the gas of a person who's just eaten an egg or the wick of a lamp that's left burning too long. Sometimes, I think that Auntie knows everything. If Mama dies, Auntie will be the first to screech.

Mama is smarter and more patient than me. She'd smile at Auntie and say: *If I had an egg, I'd give it to you.* Her lips would stretch back over white teeth. Mama could hear the first beat of a noise, just before a hen got wound up to cluck. Her hand was always ready to dip into the box and clutch around a feathered head when she heard the roll of an egg. Her fingers would nip the beak shut so no tell-tale squawk would bubble out and spill around the hut. Mama knew how to lift her shoulders, how to raise her hands and shrug in reply to Auntie's look. *Nothing*, she'd say with the white roll of her eye, while her lips stretched.

It's not hard to teach a hen. It prefers to stay silent and look at its egg, rather than have its beak nipped.

There's a piece of cloth across the door of the hut. I know it well from when I was small. I twirled, back then. Belly, hands, face, around in the folds: red and yellow as bright as a wing. Mama washed and washed until the colour faded. That way she kept the dust from staining it. Tonight, if I'm not too tired, if Mama doesn't need me to stay by her side, I'll take the cloth to the water and wash it again. Wet cloth stops the dirt from blowing in through the door. It helps Mama breathe a little stronger: more like a kingfisher's wings.

I lift the red and yellow to let me out and the morning light in. And just as I think I've been as quiet as a snake with a mouse in its belly, lying under a rock to hide from the sun, Mama's voice rises up in a whisper: *Egg?* she asks.

I kneel by her side and lift her head. As the water tips over her lips I whisper back: *Yes, Mama. I've got the egg. I didn't forget. But not today. And not tomorrow. It's too early. If the plan is to work, we must be patient. I remember what you said. Don't worry. I'm not afraid.*

Everyone has dreams.

The sun is as round in the sky as it ever is. The dust has started to rise at the place ahead. I'm not late and I'm not early. At the right time, without a watch like the one that glitters on the Boss Man's wrist, I'll stand in line with the rest.

The white man has the watch, but the African has the time, is what Mama says.

They never search on the way in. Not really. They run their hands over my front, or over my behind. I don't know why.

There are women ahead with big swollen breasts who they leave alone.

How's your Mama today, precious? They laugh. *We pay your Mama to work, not her little girl. Tell her she owes us for turning a blind eye. We'll be coming round to collect.*

Then I open my hand and they look at the egg. It is warm and brown against my skin. Long-cooled from the water that made it jump in the pan, but hot from the heat of the day. Hot from the sweat that almost makes it slip from my fingers and into the dirt by my feet. Down by my lumpy toes.

Eat it up today. You need to grow fat. You need to grow big enough to do a woman's work! They laugh again, but I am free to walk past.

There is a bite in the air and a strong choke-taste. No different than any other day. I take the cloth from my head and wrap it over my mouth. A loop at the back and a twist makes a nest for the egg. Not that this one will hatch. Life pops up all over the place, but not after bouncing around in a pan of boiling water: even a fly, a snake or a grown man can't survive that.

I work hard. I dig in the dirt. Sifting for pinpricks that slip through the fingers like grease, that shine like a new scoured pot. That have a heart if you look inside. Oh my legs ache! I squat. For a while that's easier, but the women look sideways like I am a lazy bones. They don't forgive, even though I am small. I have to learn to bend at the waist. To keep my legs straight and strong. To hold my body stiff through ache and pain, while my arms do the work. That's a woman's way. Each day might be lucky. Each day might bring something to make the bosses happy. A real find! But they don't expect me to find more than pinpricks. I only sift through the waste like Mama did.

If someone asked how many people work in a diamond mine, I'd know how to answer back: *Everyone.* I don't need any schooling for that.

If someone asked what a mine looks like, I'd laugh. Everyone works here, so everyone knows, so why ask? Clouds of dust, a big hole, dirt, wet mud, people, machines, fences, guns: that's what I'd say if someone was blind and had never seen what the world looks like.

If someone asked if I'd ever taken a diamond away from the mine and back to my hut, I'd shake my head. They'd have to be crazy to ask. Crazy people should be left alone and not answered, but if I was feeling sorry for them, because they should have known and must have forgotten, I might tell them about the searches on the way out. I wouldn't say about taking off my clothes because that's not right. It's OK for babies, but not once titties have started to grow: even a crazy person's Mama should have explained that.

If someone asked what the biggest diamond I had ever seen looked like, I would bite my lip like Mama told me. I would wave a little finger as if the tiny nail at the end might speak instead. That's big. That's really big for someone who doesn't go down in the ground to find. It would be a lie, but all people lie. When it comes to diamonds it's important to find them. It's important to get them as big as you can. It's important to hand them over right away in return for a smile. Because if you don't, the fences and guns and men will remind you why.

If someone asked what bumps around in the cloth tied at the back of my head, I could answer that: *An egg!* But it wouldn't be a real answer. Not a whole truth one like you'd say when you pray to God. Mama said that God wouldn't mind. He doesn't need to ask stupid questions. He can look right inside: through a cloth, through an egg, through a heart. Mama never said if he could look through mud, but if he could, we wouldn't have to search so hard for what he already knows how to find.

The egg bumps against my neck all day. It tap, tap, taps until the shell must be broken as if something wants to hatch out. My mouth is dry, but it longs for the dryness of egg yolk, the slippery wetness of white. There's a place where we are allowed to draw fresh water, but only when we are told.

Take a break, a Boss Man cries.

The women wear long skirts that can hide what they do when they squat in the mud.

The earth has a hole at its centre. I know that. Down, down, down in layers. Machines make the hole bigger. They throw up the mud. Mama says that some day the hole will get so big that it will swallow us all up. All the huts where we live will be sucked in and the village will be gone. The only things that will survive are the mosquitoes because they can fly, but they won't be happy because they'll have no one to bite. Mama says she hopes that day comes soon, but that was after she got sick. When she was well, she would never say that. She liked everything to be happy, even the mosquitoes and even Auntie, but mostly me.

At the end of the day we stand in line. We can wash the mud off our skin at the water place. Then at least I'm clean as I wait, as I unwind the scarf. As the egg rolls out and across a desk. As the Boss Man picks it up and bits of shell fall loose.

Didn't eat it again? Why do you bring an egg every day and not eat it? You'll get thin as a stick. You'll get sick like your Mama. What would she say? I hear him mutter the word *SLIM*. Even I know what that means. *You should get a test*, he says.

The egg sits on the table between us. His hand lies flat with hairs on the back. Pale as the day. He flicks a finger so the egg rolls towards me. I move my hand to pick it up, *dark as the night*, Mama would say. Every day for two weeks: the egg, his hands, the hairs, and mine, pale then dark, have been the same.

Auntie has a fire near the door to her hut. The sticks are red and the air above them waves. She has a pot on one side that boils and spits.

If only I had an egg, she mutters.

Her eyes are covered by drooping lids, but they still look through me like clouds in a darkening sky when she points her nose my way. I try to shrug like Mama does as I lift a hand to push at the red and yellow cloth. The air inside is thick with sweat. Mama lies on the mat and her eyes are open.

I'm a little better, she says.

The rims of her eyes are red. The skin on her arms is slack. There's a stain the size of a pot where her face has pressed down. The weave of the mat has patterned her cheek. The oil lamp flickers.

A little water? she asks.

The cloth from my head is filled with dust. I dip it up and down, up and down in a pan of water. Mama's skin presses down, presses back, so the bones underneath stand out. The cloth is soft in my hand as it wipes and cleans and wipes. I wish I could pass the cloth over and Mama would pop out new on the other side. *Coo, coo, coo,* to make me laugh. The way she was. The way she sang. The way her eyes sparkled. Like glass.

I tilt her lips to the edge of a cup so she can sip.

Tell me?

I know what she means. I tell each thing the Boss Man said. Each thing he did. I tell how his hands sprang with hairs and how bits of shell fell from the part-crushed egg.

Good girl. You can eat it now, she says.

If someone asked who is the most clever person, I'd say my mama every time.

If someone asked if she has such a big brain then why did she get sick, I'd say that even a clever person can't stop that. Everyone gets sick sometimes and everyone dies. Maybe not today or tomorrow, but it comes to us all some time.

If someone asked what Mama had got from having all those brains, I'd say not much, but there's more to be got.

And if they asked what that more was, I'd clamp my mouth shut because I'd already have said too much.

I creep out of the hut like a snake in the morning. Like a snake that only wants to eat enough and be left alone to sleep in the shade.

Egg?

Yes, here in my hand.

Mama raises herself up on one elbow and looks.

Not today, but soon, she says.

I nod my head. The red and yellow cloth shakes as I pass.

Auntie is stirring a pot of meal into a thick porridge that smells so good. I look away. Auntie is no family of mine. She's no family to Mama and no blood flows between our two lines. Mama thinks she's a spy. How else can she be fed and housed in a hut with a door made of wood? There are no sons or daughters to work off a debt and no man has ever looked under her dress, or, *if one has, he's run away in terror* is what Mama says. But a spy is always a danger so I must be polite.

Auntie, I can't be late. I must go now. Mama is sleeping. She's better today. Eat well. I hold my two hands together like I've been taught to pray. The egg between is hidden from Auntie's gaze. Even when I hop, skip, hop and run.

Ah, precious! Almost late! Two seconds more and I'd have to make your Mama pay. No egg? The Boss Man raises his eyebrows: he might mean yes, or he might mean no, but anyway I peel my hands apart, like skin from fruit, so he can see what I hold in the cup that they make.

Hurry, hurry. He waves me on.

The air is thick. It rises and blows. Even though the ground is wetted down with water, even though mud squeezes in between my toes and up my legs, the smell still gathers around my face. I tie the cloth round the egg, with a knot at the back of my head. I bend at the waist. My fingers slide. They are fast and can feel the bite of a different grit. Where a pinhead diamond waits to be found, with slick oil coat and white shine. Mama knows these things: some women wear stones round their necks, like a row of bites from the hatching eggs that a mango fly lays.

If someone asked what rolls around and tangles up between my braids, what would I say?

If someone asked what knocks against my neck as I work?

What cracks a shell, so the sweet-cooked scent blows out and up my nose?

But Ssssh! Don't ask me to answer. Don't ask me to tell. There's a diamond as big as the yellow heart of an egg. There's a plan that might hatch if it's kept warm and cherished. If I do exactly what Mama has told me to do. If I'm not afraid.

Mama found the diamond a few weeks ago. I had no more thoughts, between the ears on my head, than to wind round and round in the red and yellow cloth of a door back then. Mama didn't put the stone on the Boss Man's table. She didn't make him smile so he could whoop and run without looking back to her empty hand. She hid the diamond instead. Pushed it down between a wall and the water place, where the mud was soft, but no foot would step to let the hard stone press in. Each morning she lifted it up as she bent down to drink. Each evening she pushed the stone back in the earth where it belonged. A lot can be hidden under a woman's long skirt when she squats in the mud.

Buying time. Just buying time, Mama said. She didn't talk about what other things the diamond might buy, but her eyes shone and her mouth stretched to show her teeth. She didn't sing aloud, because secrets aren't safe. Not with Auntie just the throw of a ball of mud away. But when Mama got sick, I had to take her place. A lot can be hidden in a cloth that's wound over a mouth and tied at the back of a neck. A lot can be hidden when people think that a lump is just an egg.

You didn't eat it again? The Boss Man says.

He doesn't speak my name. His hand doesn't touch. His eyes already wander to the next in line. He doesn't watch the machine although it watches me.

The cloth across the door doesn't hang quite straight. Auntie stretches her neck to see. The porridge is gone from her pan and the fire shows no life underneath.

A girl like you is too pretty for such hard work. Auntie laughs, but her laugh is more like the sound of the wooden door closing at the front of her hut. *Tell your Mama to send you to me. I'd find you a job where you don't have to stand up all day!*

I smile and lift my eyebrows up once as if to say yes, but nothing would make me step into her hut. Nothing would make me step where the wooden door is closed against the call of birds and the beat of moth wings.

Mama lies on her mat, but she lifts her head. She lifts it onto a hand that's propped up on an elbow. She shuffles her hip.

Tell me, she whispers, but there's strength in her breath. Where a kingfisher fluttered, now an eagle beats.

He hardly looked. He didn't touch the egg.

What more can I say? I'd make it all up if it wasn't true. I'd make it up just to see her cheeks stretch, the tongue lick round over the smile and a hand stir the sweat that shines on her face.

I'm getting stronger. It should be me, not you, that takes the risk.

Her legs won't lift her beyond the pot where she squats with my help. Her arms can't work all day.

It has to be me, I say.

I should go to the water to wash Mama's mat. I should change her clothes and wipe away the smells that make other people keep away from this place. Mama just pats my hand.

Sit, she says.

I eat half of the egg and press the rest onto her tongue. Bit by bit. So she can swallow. I mix meal with cold water and let it swell. My eyes close before it is ready to eat.

I wake early. Quiet as a beetle that rolls its egg in a ball of dung. That rolls and rolls and starts all over again if the ball rolls back. No! Quieter than that! More like a snake that is sly enough to slide where he wants. That is cunning enough to hide. I know that Mama will tell me *today is the day*. I know I must do what she asks even if my heart trembles and my voice shakes. If only the sound of my dress slipping over my neck doesn't wake her. If only the crackle of my hair winding up in a rag doesn't sneak in at her ears. The roll of my foot from heel to lumpy toe is silent. So is the lift of the red and yellow cloth. I step outside and even Auntie hasn't heard me. The wooden door is closed. No laugh like a creak, asking for eggs, or offering jobs. I could escape. I could come back in the evening with a cracked shell that's bumped all day at the back of my neck. Nothing more. I could do that. What if fear makes my hand shake?

My belly hurts with hunger. There's a pan of cold wet meal inside the hut. There's water to fetch and a cup to fill, so Mama won't have to stretch too far while I'm away. My feet have to run like a gecko, so I can do everything and still get to the mine on time. Mama doesn't ask, *Egg?* when I spill water on her hand and she wakes. She knows and so do I. I look in her eyes to find the sparkle. I look inside to the heart where her secrets still shine. She lifts her eyebrows and I lift mine. I kindle a flame.

I have to run all the way with the hot egg jumping from hand to hand.

Almost too late, precious. Almost too late.

I bend for a drink of water and wonder if this day the Boss Man might be right. Just for a moment, I hunt for the diamond that shines like a pan that's been polished with sand. My fingers slip, although they are used to sifting. Sweat rises on my skin in big rain balls. It mixes with the mud and I'm sure everyone must see. But there it is! My fingers grip. Hold firm. And flick as fast as the tongue of a snake. I tie the things that bump together in a knot at the back of my head. The cloth hides my mouth, hides my lips that tremble. Mud hides my toe-curl feet.

Shake yourself girl! No one looks your way. You're one small dot among a many, many of others. You can do this. Be brave! I try to hear what Mama would say.

As the day winds towards its end, I hear her voice again: *It's time my precious girl, be brave.*

I go to the tap to wash, but I don't push the diamond back

into the ground. I take the egg from the back of my neck and hold the stone in the palm of my hand. One, two three and it will all be over. If I hold my breath and hold the egg. Hold tight.

That egg is wasted on you. I should eat it myself, the Boss Man says. He holds out his hairy hand. I hold out mine and plop! The diamond drops into his palm. Shiny. Slick with its own special oil and with my sweat.

I swallow once. I swallow twice. My throat is dryer than egg yolk dry.

I found this, I say. *Is it good?*

What's this girl? What have you found for me? Come look everyone! It's a big one! I've got a real find here!

Oh how the Boss Man smiles. The diamond that Mama has treasured for weeks becomes his own find. As quick as a flick of a finger sorting through mud, he claims his prize. I watch his backside, broad with meals of meat and nuts and fruit. He's on his feet with his hand in the air.

Look at this! Will you look at this? I've got a beauty.

I lift the egg up from the table. Slowly, slowly I step outside. My head is down. I watch my feet walking. One step, two, the lumpy toes lead the way. I wonder now what Mama will say.

It's the end of the week and a wage is waiting at the company shop. Enough to buy some fruit, some vegetables and some meal. It's enough to pay the rent on the hut. It's enough to let us live, if we don't eat a lot. I hold my dress up like a basket. Like a nest with one egg and some food on top.

You could spare something small to go in my pot, Auntie says as I pass through the rows of huts made of iron, wood and cloth. I stop by the red and yellow and turn to look. She's stirring her pot. The stick goes round and round as the porridge sets. I could give her a green banana. I could give her a handful of beans to go in her pot. But I won't.

The cloth moves to one side with a nudge from my bum.

Well? Mama says.

How's here? I ask aloud, but I nod my head.

I'm feeling much better, Mama says. *I'd like a walk.* Her voice rises. *It will do me good to move my legs.*

I'll get the cloth, I say. *It needs a wash.*

The red and yellow pulls down into my hands. I pile the food in the middle and throw the edges over the top. It makes a bundle. Not big, not small. Mama looks pretty. She must have cleaned herself. The fever has left her eyes and her legs hold straight.

Let me lean on your arm, she says.

Auntie raises her head. She stops stirring and stares instead. It's been weeks since Mama has been outside.

Did you think I was dead? Mama calls across the dirt. *Can't a person walk without everyone staring?*

And where are you going? Auntie asks.

To visit my own mama across the village, Mama says back.

We start to walk, with Mama leaning on one arm and the bundle on my head.

Oh! I forgot! Mama leans down and whispers in my ear. I run to do what she asks. At the back of the hut is a box with two silent hens. A flicker of flame from an unquenched lamp shines down on them. I peer through the wire of the lid. I untie a string. I tip and shake and wave my hands, so the hens stretch their wings and flap. Up out of the empty door and down the road. I watch them weave between the huts, leaving prints in the dust. Full-stretched wings and yellow legs turn a corner, but before the hens disappear, something opens up in a heart, in a head, in a beak and one lets out a squawk. Auntie's mouth just hangs. Her tongue licks in and out.

Mama is heavy as she leans on my arm. The bundle is heavy on my head, but I hold it tight so it doesn't slip. We walk. One step after the other, just like Mama says. We walk past the turning that would take us to her own Mama's house. They never did like each other much, so that's no surprise.

Where are you going? A woman shouts.

To Uncle's house.

We'll never arrive. Not at Uncle's, or Auntie's, or the Boss Man's house. We'll just keep walking, one foot in front of the other: our steps making marks side by side. We'll just keep walking and walking, that's Mama's plan. Until we leave this place and the mine behind. Until we are a long way into a forest, where trees grow in a tangle, or into the mountains: up high where a bird might fly. Mama whispers about places like that. She says the world is much bigger than a mine. Much bigger than my wide-stretched eyes can see. There are people out there somewhere who don't have to dig in the dirt all day. There are people who have plenty to eat.

I try to picture the hens flapping off to the grass and green trees. I try to picture the hens making prints in a forest and the clucks as they lay eggs in a nest among leaves.

If someone asked: am I sure Mama's clever, I'd say yes to that.

If they asked why we are walking, I'd tell them how one foot can cover another's print. But I'd not tell how one diamond so big can hide another stone's glitter.

We aren't greedy people, is what Mama says.

The bundle rides on top of my head. The egg with a broken shell is safe inside. Pushed deep in the yolk is a bit of sparkle. A diamond as big as the nail on my little finger. Yes, it's as big as that!

It's big enough for our dreams, is what Mama says.

She has a plan for today. She has plans for tomorrow. She has plans for lots of days after that.

First we'll burst free like a chick from an egg, then we'll learn how to fly. That's what Mama says.

KNOCKING DOWN THE NAILS

Grandfather was a carpenter. He had a love for wood, a feel for tools, a straight eye and a heart that would have beaten forever if he hadn't decided to let go. I don't think he ever drove a nail that wasn't straight and true. He once showed me how to steam and bend a solid length of timber. There was a lesson in it at the time, but I was too young to see it then. I thought he might make me a bow, or a rocking horse. All he did was give me the piece of rough, curved wood.

'Think well on that,' he said.

Stubbornness is a genetic streak in our family. I had better games to play than thinking about a piece of wood.

I'd like to be a historian when I'm older. Someone who studies Vikings and how tanks changed the course of the First World War. It's either that, or being a writer. I'm not sure, so to play it safe I listen a lot. I hear what's being said and I write it down in a copybook that lives under my bed. It's called 'Skeletons in the Cupboard'. Recording our family history might be useful in all sorts of ways.

My Uncle Johnny was sixteen when he left home. He went to America and never came back. Aunt Miriam joined the nuns at twenty-two. I never met them, my uncle and aunt. They were just part of our family history, to be lifted out and considered from time to time, like a mental photograph album.

I often met Aunt Assumpta (don't ask: just think of a moment of piety when Gran finally came face to face with her eldest daughter ... that's family history again).

The story of Uncle Johnny is this: he wanted to go to Dublin and join a band, but Grandfather didn't want him to. There was a big bust up where Johnny took a handful of notes from the tin on the dresser, walked out of the door in his best coat and was never seen again. He phoned once, from New York, but didn't say if he'd joined a band. In fact, nobody ever said what instrument he played, or maybe if he was a singer. Family history is like that: some things get shut in the cupboard for so long that they crumble into dust in the back. My Uncle Johnny might be really famous, but our family doesn't want to know. My dad thinks Uncle Johnny took the easy way out. That he didn't have to stay here, keeping an eye on things.

The story of Aunt Miriam is this: she fell in love with the man who cleans the streets in town. He was twice her age and often smelled. Grandfather said: 'Over my dead body!' So that was that. She refused to speak another word and went to join the nuns instead. I don't know if the man ever knew she loved him. I don't know if he knew she'd stayed silent from that day to this, because of him. I still see him in the street sometimes. He doesn't seem happy or sad.

The story of Aunt Ass is this: she had a husband and lost him, so that's best not mentioned. Now she nags Dad to do things that she should do herself (that's what my Mum says anyway, but I don't know if it really counts as family history, since they aren't blood relations).

The story of my dad is this: he doesn't much like Grandfather, but he visits him every Sunday the same as Aunt Ass. He feels it's an obligation, plus, he doesn't want her to get anything more than himself.

The story of my gran is this: she's dead. She was pink and rolly, she baked round cakes, everyone loved her and she never said a word against Grandfather. That's family history, but it's not true. I heard her tell him once: 'Get the broom handle out of your backside and bend just a little, or you'll lose your whole family.'

When my gran died, there was a big crowd at the funeral. Aunt Ass was there and my mum and dad and me. My grandfather stood with earth in his hand for too long, until it became embarrassing and Dad had to give him a little nudge at the elbow, so he dropped the clod straight down onto Gran's coffin. It sat there in a lump and we all looked at it.

The rain was powerful that day. It made lakes on the ground that soaked through a hole in the side of my shoe, through my socks and around my toes. Someone said, 'tears from the sky', but I knew that no one could cry that hard. It made the lump of earth sink like a collapsing volcano.

My grandfather stared hard at that coffin. It was first-class mahogany, with polished brass handles and elaborate curlicues on each corner. I'd heard him order it.

If I hadn't been watching the volcano disappear, like spud under the force of hot gravy, or thought less about my damp toes and the trickle of rain that snailed its way down my neck, I might have seen the exact moment when Grandfather did what Gran had told him to. Somewhere between dropping the earth and the rain splattering it flat, he took the broom handle out of his backside. Or maybe he didn't take it out, what with all the people. Maybe it just curved over.

Another explanation is this: there was too much moisture in the air. It had a way of seeping in, even through his best black Sunday suit. It trickled into every pore, until his spine softened and humped forward just a little.

Whatever it was, something made him lose the rigid back and the stony look.

He had to pick his path back through the mud, rotting flowers and glass chippings, stopping for a while to rest his weight on other people's gravestones. He almost looked like he could tip over, nose-first, down into all that wetness and rot.

I played the game of trying not to tread on anyone's grave while walking backwards to the cemetery gates, so I didn't really notice the hump in his back until later, when he was drinking a hot whiskey back at the house. Then it was obvious.

I wonder if history is often like that. Someone might be doodling and doesn't quite hear when Hitler says, 'Let's invade Poland,' or maybe they've gone off to the shop when Collins gets shot. I bet they'd write about it anyway, as if they'd seen everything.

I wanted to ask him if he would straighten up again once his clothes dried out and the weight was less, but he spoke before I could.

'I miss her,' he said. The rain must have got into his eyes, because they were wet too and they weren't going to dry with the heat of the fire. It couldn't have been tears, because he never, ever cried. My dad told me that.

Then there were the arguments. Grandfather usually wanted Dad to help him when we visited on a Sunday. There was always some job that needed two pairs of hands. The problem was that Dad's hands didn't do things the way my grandfather's did.

'Give that hammer to me,' Grandfather shouted. 'If you bend that nail over any further it'll be kissing its own arse.'

'I'd like to see you sat in front of a computer,' my dad muttered back.

Gran wasn't there any more to soothe things out and make everyone friends. No one ever learned how to do that as well as her. We always ate tea in a hurry, so we could get away before my dad said anything he would regret. He said it in the car on the way home instead. Sometimes we gave Aunt Ass a spin home too and then they sniped together about how impossible Grandfather was. That's how I first heard about the coffin. After that I had to see it.

'That's a rose,' my grandfather said. 'It was the first flower I ever gave to your gran. I stole it from a garden on the way back from the dance hall. Not that I'm proud of the stealing, but I'll always remember her smile when I snapped the thorns from the stem to protect her fingers. I missed one, though. It drew a drop of blood.'

'Is that what that is?' I pointed to a spatter of drop-shapes, carved near the end, where the feet would rest.

'That's the rain at her funeral. It'll look more realistic when it's sanded and polished. I'm working through our life together, from the top down. The rose is at the head; this haystack is where we rested for a while on a hot sunny day. There'll be baby bonnets and seashells and a cross for Mass on Sundays.' He shook his head. 'Her whole life was a series of small moments. But she strung them together like the finest pearls. She wore them in her smile, in her hands as they baked bread and in her soft breath as she slept. I just didn't appreciate her the way I should have.'

'Is that her eyes?' I asked, as I pointed to two bumps just taking form along one side. He didn't answer.

'Pearls,' he said. 'A whole life of pearls and I never saw what a precious jewel she was until she was gone.'

Some things need writing down just the way they were said.

'It's ridiculous,' my dad said on the way home. 'She died six months ago, what's the point in carving a coffin for her now? I hope he doesn't plan to have her disinterred.'

'We'd soon put a stop to that,' Aunt Ass said. 'It's obscene and I'm sure it's against the law as well.'

Sometimes adults don't know anything.

'It's not for Gran,' I told them. 'It's for himself. He wants to be buried with Gran wrapped all around him. It's the stories of their life together. Like pearls on a necklace.'

'Your gran never had any pearls! She had a bully of a husband who always thought he knew what was best. A coffin for himself indeed!'

It was for him, though. I knew that, because Grandfather had told me. I think, in a way, he wanted to say sorry to Gran.

Sometimes things have to get worse before they get better. It's a thing my dad says. Aunt Ass and him had a real go at my grandfather:

'It's not decent, carving a coffin like that. Are you going to put it in the bedroom and just hop in when you think the time is right?' That was Aunt Ass.

'Of course it's a work of art, Dad, but a lot of people won't see it that way. You can't have a pair of breasts on the side for all the world to see.' That was my dad.

'She had beautiful bosoms. They were good enough to feed you. They are fine enough to grace my coffin.' That was Grandfather.

'Well, you'll have no say in it! You'll be gone and we'll put you where we want.'

'You'll get nothing from me, if you do.'

'I don't want anything from you, if I have to be shamed in the process!'

'You always have to do things the way you want. You've no thought for anyone else.'

Stubborn, the whole lot of them.

Dad wouldn't leave it alone.

'I won't go to the funeral,' he said to my mum.

'You won't get the hall table,' she replied. She knew how badly he wanted it.

'I won't get it anyway, with Assumpta on the case.'

He was right, we all knew it.

'Johnny won't be there and nor will Miriam. They got themselves well away and never looked back. There'll be no tables for them.'

'You'll go for your dad's sake,' my mum said. 'You're a proud man, just like him. But if you don't go, you'll never forgive yourself. There'll be no second chance.'

'That's exactly the way he is: no second chances. If he decides you're wrong, then you're wrong. That's that. He won't bend for anyone. Don't think we haven't tried to make him see sense.'

We had a wet June and an even wetter July. August brought rain so severe that half of Grandfather's front path was washed away. The wetness seemed to eat at him, until his eyes were constantly staring at his knees and his back hurt with trying to straighten. I caught one glimpse of the coffin, when he asked me to bring a hammer up from the shed. It was polished and oiled, almost wet itself in its beautiful slickness. I sneaked a look and the boobs were there, sure enough, with nipples and all. There were words too, like 'fidelity' and 'regret', all crisply incised. I was probably the last person, other than himself, to see it.

I think this was an important point in our family history.

I don't know when he decided. I don't know when he did the act or what really convinced him. October was cold and bright, leading into a winter that froze ice on the inside of the windows. Most Sundays, Grandfather was lying in bed, all curled up and breathing heavily when we arrived.

'He shouldn't be alone,' Aunt Ass said.

'He'd hate to be anywhere else,' my dad replied.

I'm sure Grandfather could hear them from behind his door.

I'm not ashamed that I stole the key. Sometimes historical research is important. I honestly wasn't going to look at the boobs.

I let out a shout at the sight of it. All the carving was gone. Chipped away. Leaving a rough surface like waves in a squall.

'I made it to celebrate our time together. I wanted to feel she would always be with me. I needed to say with my hands how much she meant to me. Somehow, I never seemed to find the words,' my grandfather sighed. 'But not everything in life goes the way you want it to and there are few choices that go hand in hand with death. You just can't hurt the ones you leave behind.'

I hadn't believed until then, that my grandfather was leaving.

'But it was your coffin,' I said. 'You spoilt it just because Dad and Aunt Ass didn't like it.'

'Even the most rigid of us can bend if we have to,' he sighed, and his breath was a rattle. 'Your gran always knew that. All we need is some force that can get right inside; that can turn us pliant, where once we refused to move. Stubbornness is a curse in our family. Don't carry it through into your generation. I carried it for too long in mine.'

My grandfather died at 9.35 p.m. I noted it down.

When, the right prayers had been said and the doctor had done his bit, there were only the three of us left: Assumpta, my dad and me.

'Let's do it ourselves,' my dad said. So we lifted Grandfather into the coffin.

He wasn't heavy at all. The waves, where a gouge had stroked, washed around him. He lay there and we just looked. I hadn't noticed before, how there was a slight curve, a banana shape, to my grandfather's box. His bent body fitted in as neat as a bean is embraced in its downy soft pod.

I was bawling. My dad kept blowing his nose. The tears sloshed down Assumpta's face; even she was softened. It doesn't take much to bend, once the process is started. We all looked at the coffin with its wiped-out story of my grandfather's love, my grandfather's life. We stood there, bowed down, wet-faced and forgiving. The stubbornness flowed out from the generations, leaving us awash in a puddle of generosity.

'You take the hall table,' Aunt Ass said.

'No. You have it,' my dad replied.

They offered and accepted, gave and gave again: the table, the clock, the sideboard, the wedding photo that nobody really needed. The proceeds from the house would be split down the middle.

'He wouldn't know,' Aunt Ass said, as her tears dried. 'If we ordered a coffin today: best mahogany, to match Mum's?'

A stubborn streak can be really useful. I stopped crying for long enough to have my say. 'No way!' I shouted.

Dad nodded. 'No way,' he said too. 'We'll put on the lid and I'll knock down the nails. Some things are wrong and some things are right.'

My grandfather had drilled small holes to guide the shafts down. Dad knocked all the nails home, straight and true.

Historical footnote:

My dad is still stubborn when it suits him, but he has booked a ticket to America to visit Uncle Johnny (who plays the fiddle). He wasn't impossible to find, once Dad put his mind to it.

Aunt Ass got the hall table and most of my grandfather's furniture, even though, by rights, some of it belonged to Dad.

Aunt Miriam is still silent within her order.

And me? I think history can be too hard to write down. You have to be truthful whether you want to or not. I didn't fully respect my grandfather's wishes to end the genetic thing with my generation. I felt he deserved to have some things the way he wanted, so I slipped an envelope into his coffin, before we closed it down and got on with our lives. In it were pictures I had drawn in pencil and coloured with crayons: a rose, a haystack, a really huge pair of boobs and a necklace glowing with pearls.

A Fair Trade

The door to the range is ajar. It lets heat into the room, but only a little. Last night's logs are burned down to embers and the ones that will kindle the morning haven't yet caught light. A flicker would do. Sheila knows she could bend and blow, or flap a piece of cardboard torn from a box. Anything that pushes air into the cooling remains of the fire would make a flame snap. But the tea is hot in her cup: she'd have to put it down and risk bending forward if she wanted to blow or to flap.

Blackness presses its weight against the window. The house is too many miles from a street lamp and more miles again from anywhere that the sun has already started to rise. It always seems to get darker in the hour before the sun hauls up a new day's light.

The toes of Sheila's socks need darning. That's a word she wouldn't have known three years ago, but now she's quite adept. Not fine cotton socks, but the thick ones that keep feet warm in a pair of rubber boots. The wool never lasts long when it's rubbed between boot and skin. The heels and the toes go first, while there's still plenty of wear left in the rest. It's Sheila's choice as to the colour of wool she'll use. It brightens up grey socks to put red at the toe and yellow wrapped round the heel. She's quite fond of orange rising up the back of the leg.

Peter brought her here three years ago. It's the exact date of the anniversary. He might not remember, but Sheila does. The darkness doesn't seem to bother him, but then he'd been reared to it. The same way he'd been reared to sit up all night with a calving cow and only an oil lamp for company. Then again, he'd been reared to expect a wife to cook and clean for the men; to mind chickens and children: the first for money, the second to help on the land.

It's all in the rearing. She couldn't blame him for that. It's all in the expectations that anyone is brought up to have.

Sheila was brought up where street lamps make the night sky glow. The light hangs like a toxic cloud whenever they drive in from the west. As soon as she dips back in at the edges, her heart starts to race, but they can't go back often – it isn't easy to get someone to mind the farm. There are always new things being born and losses that might be incurred. There is always some field to cut, or a ditch to clear. The breaks in the fencing eat through coils of wire, some barbed and some plain.

The mountains are to blame. They block out the sun, so light comes late and goes early. Peter told her that before they moved back, but then she had thought mountains beautiful and long nights romantic. Now she complains as much as he does – how you can't live off land that looks pretty but is covered in stone. Both of them long for more sleep.

They'd met when they were at college, where things like last names and what parents did for a living weren't mentioned. She'd called him Pete and only added the r when they moved back to his homeplace. It was some strange confusion between the death of his parents and respect for the full name they had given their son. Of course she'd known about the farm when they married. The whole clan of aunts, uncles and cousins had come up from the country for a couple of days and she'd visited them a time or two as well. What she hadn't understood was how deep the vein of tradition ran. How a car crash could kill his parents and put a pull on Peter's heart that would turn both of their lives around.

How foolish she'd been at the time of the accident! Somewhere deep down – where guilt hid the notion, because no one should look at gains at a time of such loss – she'd wondered how much Pete would inherit. She'd wondered what forty acres of hill farm was worth. Would a small flat of their own be possible? If Pete's wage as a computer repair man was put alongside hers as a junior aide in PR? But she'd learned that a farmer has the grit of the land in his blood. In fact he'd more willingly cut a wrist and let some drops run, than part with a small field full of bracken where the sheep won't bother to graze.

The fire spits as it catches. A spark flies and singes the wool of her sock. It's soon extinguished, but the smell lingers on. She should push the fire door shut. That way it will draw better and a steady heat will build in the iron casing. But there is something that holds her to the bright flame and the small warmth that reaches out just as far as her knees and hands. Peter says they will put in a back boiler and fit central heating, or maybe he'll even look into getting an oil tank. Sheila knows that won't happen. Not as long as he frowns each night at the computer on the corner of the table and tries to balance the accounts. If it wasn't for the government grants, they would never make enough to see to bills and their immediate needs. There are neat piles of dockets, paid and unpaid, on the table. A paperweight with snow and a penguin sits on the ones they still owe. That way, their debts can't blow off the table in a draught and be ignored. Peter is meticulous about that kind of thing.

There are lines round his eyes when he walks in the door.

'A bull calf,' he says. 'They're both on their feet. He's sucking hard. A strong young thing.'

'There's tea in the pot. Will I fry an egg?'

'Don't worry, I'll do it. You must be tired yourself,' he says.

Sheila's knees ache. That was something she never knew before recent weeks. Once, she could dance half the night and be back on her feet for work in the morning without a pain.

Now her eyes are gritty with tiredness and her back, belly and knees make her feel twice her age.

'I'm sorry,' she says.

'Ah love! What for? It'll get easier, you'll see. You're doing so well!'

'Not half as good as that cow! Will you buy in another calf to rear on the milk? Imagine if she could feed two …'

'We don't have the grass for that,' he says.

Three years ago, Sheila would have wondered what he meant. Now she knows all about the big farms up the country that can rear beef as easy as watching grass grow. She knows that their own farm is good for nothing but sheep. They'll rear the calf for a while then sell him on. They'll use the milk themselves after that and put the cow back to a bull as soon as they can.

'It's quiet,' Peter says. 'You should catch up on sleep.'

Sheila nods as if she agrees. Sleep is important. Everyone knows that. But so is a bit of time to herself, when she can read a magazine, or even put on a bit of makeup. Her hair feels limp.

'You need sleep too,' she says. He nods back as if he agrees, but he doesn't get up from the table when he finishes the eggs. He pushes the plate aside and looks under the penguin. The bird's feet are lost in a flurry of snow.

'We could sell a field or two, Peter. Just to pay the bills and to get us set up. If you bought a new tractor and mended the shed. And the heating maybe. We'd never forgive ourselves if anything happened because of the cold.'

'There's no need for cold,' Peter sighs. He takes her hand in his own. He holds it as carefully as when he moved the still-blind kittens to a drier place in the shed. 'We've plenty of wood, don't spare it. I'll fill up the basket whenever you want. We've a dry house and you can plug in the electric heater to take the chill off a room. I'll mend the tractor, and the tin that blew from the roof of the shed can soon be put back. It's only a few bales of hay that got wet. You know I'd never forgive myself for being the one to split up the farm.'

It's always the same. They get so far, then no more is said. If she pushed, Sheila might get him to change his mind. They might move back to the city and pick up on old lives, but she knows that isn't an option. A man who has to choose between the love of his wife and the love of his land will never be happy once that choice is made.

'I could ask Ma for a loan?' she says.

'I'd sooner go to the bank than have your Ma breathing down my neck.' Peter smiles, but Sheila knows he's not joking. Her ma runs a corner shop like she's the head of a prison: no one escapes without paying their dues.

'Heaven help us if we couldn't pay her back,' she says.

The smile is real now. It reaches up to Peter's eyes and makes them shine. He drops a kiss on the top of her head.

'I know it seems hard right now. But it will get easier. You'll get stronger. I've done the projections and if we only do well with the lambing, we'll pull through.'

'Could we not try Organic?' Sheila asks. She remembers when it was the thing to do as a student. When they joined the Greens and paid over the odds for a block of Fair Trade chocolate with no chemicals used in production at all. It was best for the farmers and for the people that ate it, they'd agreed. She'd sucked each square of chocolate slowly, trying to savour all that she could from each piece. Now, she shops where things are cheapest. It's the price of each tin, that bothers her, not the growing of the beans.

'I think we should, Peter. I do. I think we should.' The strength of feeling grabs her, making her gasp. 'It's not just for the extra grant. It's because of us. It's because of him!'

Her voice rises. A thin, high cry floats down the stairs to meet it.

'It's a lot of work and what would we use instead of the sheep dip? You've not seen what happens when fly gets into the wool. It's not pretty. We'll not make any hasty decisions, Sheila. Stay where you are. You shouldn't lift.'

The line on her belly still hurts. In the night she thought she'd burst a stitch. How could she not lift when the baby was hungry and Peter was out with the cow in the shed? The crying is loud from such a tiny thing. He doesn't sleep well, her child, as if her milk is too thin, or there isn't enough.

Tears prick the back of her eyes, but that happens all too often these days. She could cry at the sight of a calf, or a broken tractor, as easy as at that of her man in his old Aran jumper carrying their first born in his arms.

'He's a hungry boy,' Peter says.

Sheila can hitch her blouse out of the skirt and hoist it. Or, she can unfasten a button or two and pull down the neckline. One shows more of these new blue-lined breasts that she's invented, but the other reveals the bandage that holds her belly in place. There's something about the high-pitched crying that frays all the edges. She pulls at the blouse, snapping buttons and revealing the new body that marks her from neck to waist.

Soft lips latch onto tender nipples. Sheila flinches and wonders how long it can be like this? Each tug pulls something from her. Each suck makes her dread that the nipple might split. Would she feel different if he'd been born in a natural way? If she'd pushed him out roaring instead of having him plucked from her womb in silence, while she felt no pain?

'Will I do the nappy?' Peter says.

Sheila knows that a farmer's wife should be pushing out babies and feeding hens. She should be out on the roof nailing up tin. She should be thinking of ways to save the farm. 'Can people change?' she asks.

That's enough to set the tears rolling. They drip from her cheeks onto the soft blanket. One lands on the tiny hand.

'You'll feel better in a few days,' Peter says. 'This will pass. Nothing is ever as bad as it seems.'

The days escape her in a blur of sucking and sleeping; of tiny nappies that still seem too big to fit the tinier waist. Ma comes for a visit and leaves with a camera full of photographs. She wants to pin them to the board behind the till in the shop.

'People ask!' she says. She talks about routine and being cruel to be kind. 'In my day people left a fussy baby to cry. You need your sleep too,' she says.

Ma tidies the drawer that holds the cutlery and sweeps the spiders from under the bath. She suggests that a new doormat would be in order, but there's never a quiet moment where Sheila could mention a loan.

'You didn't, did you?' Peter asks. 'Well, I'm glad about that.'

His words might be hasty. The bank refuses another loan without any new venture to base it on. They're getting tighter about pouring money into acres of land that are only suited to raising stones.

Sheila's belly shrinks, the wound heals and her nipples grow harder. She learns to bake bread with a child tied against her. The calf goes off to the mart and the cow's udder swells. It's hard not to identify with the beast, as Sheila squats to draw off the milk.

Peter sits in the evenings before the computer, but he doesn't play games. The pile under the penguin has grown bigger and the lower field has flooded with all of the rain.

'You're right,' he says, as she peels back the tabs on a nappy. 'I'm stupid to put us all through this. I thought I could make this place work, the same as my father and his father did. But did I ever know what sacrifices they made? What did my father have to do to put me through college? What did he and Mammy have to do to live in a place like this?'

'They borrowed,' she said. 'That's why you started out with a farm that's drowning in debt.'

'But they were never extravagant! There were no holidays or fancy clothes. When my father bought a car he ran it for ever. And it still looked as shiny at the end, as it did on the day he first got it.'

'And what about them?' Sheila says. 'Did they keep their shine?'

Peter looks like she's hit him. She can't bear to see that in his eyes. She wants to smile, to push back her hair with a shake, as if she's still the same shiny person that once bought Fair Trade.

He hits the table with the flat of his hand. 'You can't eat land,' he says. 'I'll sell a field, or two, to pay off the bank and maybe another one to put us ahead.'

The baby kicks his legs. A pulse flutters at his temple. The fontanelle shares the beat, beneath the soft fuzz of hair on the top of his head. Sheila's finger traces where fine lines stretch beneath the fragile skin.

'It's blood that links us all,' she says.

'It's not a good time to sell,' the Estate Agent pronounces. An engineer comes to plot the land. 'It's not much of a site. No hope of mains water, or sewerage,' he shakes his head. 'Maybe if you included the flat field over there?'

'What would be left to farm?' Peter says.

In the evenings they sit by the stove. The house has warmed as the days get longer and there's no need to leave the fire door open, but it's a comfort to watch the flames. The baby pulls on Sheila's hair as he sucks. His fingers twirl beneath the strands. His blue eyes follow where her head moves.

'Lambing will start soon enough,' Peter says. 'We'll pick up a bit on that and the feeding will drop once the grass starts to grow.'

'Does everything come back to grass?' Sheila asks.

She tries making cheese. The milk sets into a thick white curd. She cuts it and stirs. The first cheese tastes of nothing much. To the next one she adds a few chives. It's better, but Peter says to let it ripen for longer. The outside turns green and blue on her third attempt. The fourth one is left uncovered and she won't eat anything where a fly might have laid eggs.

'So much for our cheese empire,' Peter laughs.

There's a job in the town. It's on a checkout: just twelve hours a week it says in the ad.

They talk about Peter minding the baby, maybe weaning the infant onto solid food. The wage can't be much, but maybe it would help if Sheila spent a few hours out of the house. She looks in the cupboard for clothes for an interview. There are plenty to choose from; none of them worn since she came to the farm. Her feet remember the snug grip of high heels. She can't believe how her pulse beats as she drives into town.

But there's more snap to Sheila's dress than that of the manager who interviews her. She should have known that her roots in Ma's shop were more important for this than a sharp pair of heels.

'Don't cry, love,' Peter says. 'There'll be other jobs.'

The table is covered in papers. One is a map that shows boundaries in red, wrapped round the edges of the best flat field.

'I'm phoning Ma,' she says.

At the back of her mind, Sheila has always believed that her mother is a rock. A place to clamber and sit that will be safe from the storms. She knows that if she could only get over her own reservations and ask, then her mother will come through with a cheque. There will be conditions and strings, that's the problem, but she never doubts that her mother has plenty of money sitting comfortably in the bank. In her head, Sheila dreads asking the question, but hearing the answer is harder again.

'I'm sorry, Sheila. You know I would if I could. There's no money in a small shop these days. Not with all the big new ones, where things cost less and less. The bank were all too willing to lend at one time, but now they aren't listening when I say times are hard. I'm thinking of selling, to pay them off.'

Peter just nods his head when Sheila tells him. 'We're all the same,' he says.

The wound on her flesh has healed months before, but something infects her belly none the less. It burns like a fire that has just been kindled.

'Ma's not selling her shop and you're not selling this land,' she says. Her heels click as she walks out of the door. They stick down in the mud of the lower field and almost twist her over on her ankle where the ground is strewn with stones. Her snappy dress is out of place amongst the bracken, but her head is focused and thinking and in the right space. The river bends into a natural pool flanked with trees. Small walls snake round pretty fields. There are slabs laid as bridges over streams. There's a mountain that reaches tall and majestic into the clear air.

'We're good people, you and me, Peter,' she says, as she walks back in the door. There's mud up the side of her ankle and a rip in her tights where a thorn has snagged. In her right hand she hefts a stone from the mountain.

'We don't deserve what's happening. But if we lie down, then they win. They take everything we've got and there's nothing left to pass on to him.'

The baby smiles with a wide open mouth. He chuckles and flaps his hands.

'What's on your mind?' Peter says.

'Your family loved this place. You do too. My ma loves her shop. I love the whole lot of you. Love like that should move mountains. They say you can't eat rock, but you can.'

Peter spends hours in front of the computer. Sheila pays the phone bill and nearly wears out the buttons with all of her calls. She's up and dressed for work in the mornings. Her brain ticks off plans as she walks the floor with her baby in the middle of the night. Most impressive of all, she persuades the bank to back off and even to extend the debt. Her new venture tickles the mind of the manager, but the fire in her eyes is what guarantees the loan.

There's nothing too strange about going organic. There's nothing too strange about taking advice and getting the grant.

There's nothing too hard about keeping sheep healthy, or growing potatoes and beans on a flat piece of land. There's nothing strange about a baby sitting on the earth and pulling at a worm with his hands. What is strange is the other half of the plan and the fact that Sheila's ma goes along with it.

There are photographs on the board behind the till in Ma's shop. There are forms to fill in. Then there's Ma with her arms waving and pointing; telling any interested person just what the deal is. She's as good as a warden of any prison, but here the act doesn't have to be committed beforehand, if someone just thinks that they might, then she hauls them in.

'Anyone can do their bit,' she says.

She has a pile of stones on the counter. Each one is for sale, at a price. The pictures on the wall are of the bend in the river, the farmhouse and the mountain behind. The shop's got a name for being 'crazy organic'. It sells wine, rice, shirts, back scratchers and herbs. It sells a few vegetables like beans and potatoes. Before too long there might be leeks and lamb.

'It works like this,' Ma says to a young man and woman who stand at the counter. 'You pay me enough to cover the costs of a holiday up in the mountains: it's not much, just enough to keep you fed and warm for the week. You work for four days out of the seven and for the rest you can do what you want.

You don't have to be an expert in anything. There are fields to be drained and stones to be picked off the land. For each week of work I give you one of these.' She holds a stone in her hand. 'It's an investment. A bit like gold. It says: who needs banks? It says: I believe in the land. It says: I believe in a promise made by a decent woman and an honest man.'

'Wow! That's a lot to put on one stone,' the young man laughs.

'It is, so instead it just says: One Day! Here read it yourself. You can redeem the stone in different ways. It's a token, or permit if you like, that says you can go for a swim in a pool in the mountains whenever you want. Or you can trade it for vegetables, or meat, when the field that it's pulled from begins to crop. Some people just like to use them as paperweights, or doorstops. It's what it reminds them of that matters, they say. We have to all pull together in times like this.'

Ma's doing well enough for herself with the new line of goods. People will travel a way through the city for her special brand of Organic Fair Trade.

Sheila sits by the range. She can see the flame. There's an open fire through in the parlour and a row of rubber boots by the door. Baby Joe runs between the rooms, showing off to the visitors. Someone blows a stream of rainbow bubbles while he tries to clap them between his hands. Everyone loves her child. Everyone loves what they know of her life.

New people have arrived today. They'll sleep in the shed that's reroofed and converted. They'll start out as visitors and end up as friends. Most likely they'll come back again and again. Most amazing of all, it seems there's cachet in having a pile of ONE DAY! stones in a city garden, or lined up on a balcony high above a street.

Peter is tapping away on the computer. Other farmers want to know the secret of eating rocks. There's talk of a larger, co-operative venture; maybe even grants.

'We aren't wealthy, but the projections are sound and we meet so many good people. Life is rich,' he writes.

The penguin sits on a shelf near the door. It's seldom disturbed enough to whirl up the snow at its feet. Bills are paid when they come in if they possibly can be.

'We're never again building up debts,' is what Peter says.

Sheila stitches red wool to the heel of a sock. Maybe she'll put green on the toe. She could buy more socks instead of stitching, but she's grown to like the dip and pull of bright wool: drawing the raw edges together and filling in the spaces between. Outside in the yard the chickens are thriving. The city people love the eggs and always like to take a few back home. Ma can sell the rest.

The fire in Sheila's belly that burned long enough and strong enough to fuse her dreams with reality, has been replaced by the slow growing heat of new flesh and bone. Soon, she'll tell Peter. She'll find a quiet moment when the visitors are asleep and the darkness presses against the windows. She'll push her belly to his back, so she can feel his heartbeat and he can feel hers.

'Can we afford a new child in the house next spring?' she'll say.

He'll worry for her health, but that won't stop her: 'I'm a farmer's wife now. Just look at the chickens. Just look at Joe. Just look at the good man I have as a husband. And think of the grit in the blood that links us all. Maybe this birth won't live up to my expectations. Maybe the doctors will have to slit open my belly to pull this child out too. Maybe I'll weep, I don't know. Maybe the farm will fail and the bank will fore-close and no amount of rocks shipped off to the city will stop them. But I don't think so.'

Sheila lifts the length of wool to her teeth and bites it. The darning is neat. The socks will last for a good while longer. She smiles as she rolls them one into another to make a tight ball.

FISHING FOR DREAMS

My father lived on a boat at the bottom of the lawn. There was a river there. A slow, sluggish affair that puddled with brown warm pools as much as any swirls and eddies. My mother put up a screen to shield the view. She painted some panels pink and some panels blue to remind her of flowers. She said the sight of that old tub offended her. Sometimes I thought she meant the boat. Other times I knew she meant my father.

I'd peep around the screen to see if he was still there. He'd smile if he saw me, but I would hide my face and only open my eyes behind my fingers. It was hard keeping true to Mother, and harder still not to run towards the water and stretch my arms around his belly. Most of the summer, I sat behind the screen and wished with all my mind to take us back to a time when the river didn't have a boat and the only tub my mother talked of was in the bathroom.

My father always liked the water. Even before the boat or the screen appeared, he'd hold my hand and we'd walk down to the river. It didn't bother him to sit all day with a line played out on the water and a cap tilted down on his forehead. I played with the big old net that was supposed to scoop out a fish, but was more use for dredging the edges and sifting through weed.

'Let's see who gets one first,' my father said.

I dredged. He sat. Sometimes he'd jump to his feet and shout that I'd just missed a big one!

'Keep looking,' he'd say. 'It might come back.'

I don't think I ever saw a fish in that river. I don't remember my father pulling one up from the depths on a line. I don't know what a man who preferred to stick a lump of bread on the hook than to harm a worm would have done with a live, hurting, wriggling fish.

We'd walk back across the lawn when the midges started to bite.

'You won again,' he'd say. He meant that the fish that I hadn't seen had been bigger than anything he hadn't caught. I was happy then. Much happier than if I'd had a flapping wet fish in a plastic bag.

I don't know what my mother did while we were away. Or, at least, I knew one thing. The fish fingers would be browning in the frying pan and the bottle of tomato sauce would be out on the table when we got back. She didn't go out, because she couldn't drive and my bike was too small for her to ride.

'Did you have a good day?' my father always asked.

She'd nod her head, while I talked about what I'd done. What I'd seen. Like the snail that climbed right up a blade of grass, until the stem bent over and touched back down to the ground.

'Do you think it does that same thing all day?' I asked. 'Is it trying to reach the sky? Does it feel sad when it finds itself back down on the ground? Do snails get bored with just being snails?'

My father said, 'Hush.'

I wondered why talk of that snail made my mother cry.

'I'm sure it was pretty. Probably the prettiest snail on the whole riverbank,' my father said. He reached out to try to touch my mother's skirt, but she made a dash for the sink and started to wash dishes even though we hadn't quite finished.

It wasn't. Pretty that is. It was just an ordinary snail, the same as a hundred others, but I didn't say so.

My father sailed home in the boat a few days after that. If the snail made my mother cry, then the boat turned on a tap so she couldn't stop.

'How could you?' she said. 'We have little enough to live on! There's no chance of a new dress, or a trip to the cinema. What about the school uniform? She can't start school in a pair of old dungarees!'

Mother probably didn't say more because I was there. She might have muttered: 'That's the final straw,' because that was something that she often said. She walked out of the room each time my father tried to speak.

I don't exactly remember how, but my mother stayed in the house and my father went to live on the boat. The screen was put up part way between them, but it didn't really hide him. Not if I went upstairs and looked out of a window. Not if I leaned out and waved. Sometimes he waved back and sometimes his cap was tipped down on his forehead, so he couldn't see. I wanted to run down the lawn and to pick up the net. If he caught a fish he'd have no one to help him! But I knew that I wasn't supposed to visit the tub – whichever of them my mother might mean.

Maybe Mother wished she could run down too. I saw her sometimes hiding behind a curtain while she pretended to squash flies at an upstairs window. She didn't wave, but she did look out towards the water. She talked about planting something to flower across the screen in the autumn and something to burst through in the following spring. That gave me hope! If my father could burst through that screen, then maybe things would go back to the way they were. But he had other plans.

My mother sat out in the garden. The sun boiled down all over the place, but the screen made a patch of shade. Her face was tilted up. Her eyes were closed, so she didn't see what was coming. A thin point rose up above the top of the boards. Above the blue and the pink. It was the tip of a fishing rod. I knew that straight away, but it kept on rising. My mother didn't open her eyes until she felt something brush against her face.

It was a fish finger held in place by a safety pin. My father wouldn't run the risk of harming anything.

'Oh that's cold!' my mother said. She jumped to her feet.

'It's not been fried! It's just come from a fridge,' I shouted. I danced and tried to catch the end of the line.

'Or from the bottom of the river,' my father's voice floated over the fence. It was deep and wobbly as if his belly shook.

'I've come to invite you both to share in my catch. I caught a whole packet. There's plenty for all, if you want to come down to the boat for tea?'

I held my breath. The line didn't sway. The fish finger floated in front of my mother's face.

'Tom, you're a fool and you always will be,' she said. 'But you can't live off foolishness. You can't eat dreams.'

I wanted to point out that you could eat fish fingers and this one was real enough, but I didn't think that was what she meant.

'I know you've been down,' my father said.

Well, that wasn't fair! My mother had told me not to go down to the boat, so why should she?

'I know you're depressed and it's my fault. I know I play the fool, but now I'm serious. I want to make things right,' he said.

'What's serious about a fish finger on the end of a line?' my mother asked. She put out a hand and snapped, so the flying fish was caught in her fingers.

'I'm just fishing for dreams,' my father said. 'I have high hopes for the perfect catch.'

Slowly, with the tick, tick, tick of the reel going round, he drew her in.

'Quick! Get the net!' he shouted. But I'd already thought of that. I ran round that screen as fast as a fish could flip.

The old net lay on the ground at my father's feet. There was a hole to one side and a bit of the rim was bound with string. Slowly, slowly, he reeled my mother round to his side of the screen. He pulled so her tummy touched against his. He kissed her on the lips.

'That's better than kissing a fish,' he whispered. He winked, so I knew what to do next. I jumped in the air and flipped up the net. It was big. Big enough, and more so with the hole to stretch it, to come over both their heads. To trap them forever in a kiss.

'How could you buy a boat?' my mother said. 'When things are so tight? When anything we might reach for is beyond our grasp? When we struggle so much just to survive?'

'I didn't pay for it!' he laughed. 'Not with money anyway. It was badly holed. There was a lot of rot. I worked a few extra hours at the yard in return for the wood. I patched it up. It cost nothing to sail it here and it will cost nothing to sail it away. If that's what you want it'll go in the morning.'

My mother breathed out into his face. He closed his eyes as if her breath smelt as nice as the flowers that might grow one day on the other side of the screen.

'Will you take this net away, child!'

It tangled in my mother's hair, but she laughed as it came loose. She caught my hand and my father held one too. We walked down across the lawn. The grass was long because no one had bothered to cut it, but that was nice, because snails could climb much nearer to the sky. The droop of the bending stalk would be almost like flying.

My father swung me up over the edge of the boat, as if I was as light as a fishing line. He jumped up himself and put down a hand. My mother climbed slowly up the boards that clad the side. He held an arm at her waist to balance the gentle rock and sway. So she wouldn't fall down.

'Take a look at the cabin,' my father said. He held out a hand to stop me from following. 'It's your mother I have to persuade,' he whispered. 'You stay up here and keep an eye on the ties, so we don't drift away. And keep an eye out for fish!'

Over the edge, the brown water slapped at the wooden

planks. Weed slung its arms out every which way. Insects dipped and hovered at the still points, and leaves dropped slowly from the row of golden trees. I closed one eye and counted. I stared at just one leaf and said one, two, three, until it had floated from one end of the boat to another. Just like a duck in the bath that I pushed, watched and counted until it tipped against my feet. But this took much longer than that. I said his words over and over, until they became an answer: 'Don't drift away, don't drift away, drift away, drift away ...' My eyes almost closed into sleep.

My father lived on a boat at the bottom of the lawn and so did my mother and me. We could untie a knot, or lift off a loop. We could release all the strings and float away. We could leave behind all the worries, all the snails and the screen that was painted blue and pink. What else did we need, but the boat and the river, the rod and the line, and a net that once caught a dream? What did we need as long as we were all together, like tubs in a tub, with fish fingers to be fried for tea?

Someone was big enough to work out all the knots and how to release them without too much hurt, but I swear, it wasn't me.

EVERY CLOUD

Some people say that a glass is half full and others that it's half empty, but Miriam can't see either point of view. A half-full glass can be drunk until it's dry and a half-empty one can soon be topped up. Where's the problem? It's what's contained by the glass that matters: how it swirls round and colours the sides with amber; how there's still the faint memory of a burn at the back of the throat as it slides down and how it holds a promise of what's to come. The best things in life are like that: they meet expectations, no matter what you ask.

Miriam isn't supposed to drink. Not today. But there's nothing to say that she can't find comfort in a thought. In fact, there's a lot to be said for closing her eyes and picturing the pour, the swirl, the lift, the burn.

'Just like a Russian gymnast,' she laughs aloud.

A gymnast! Now there's a thought she can't begin to conjure! Her breasts would beat like gongs, if she ever had the strength to twirl around the asymmetric bars. She blames age for that. Somewhere between forty and fifty, Miriam woke to the realisation that muscle had turned to fat and the pull of gravity could only be combated by bigger knickers and bigger bras. She'd bought bigger hats as well as jackets that were broad at the shoulder and blouses with bits that dangled to hide any recalcitrant bulge. Not that she'd ever wanted to be a gymnast, but she could claim a long-held interest in bars.

She'd watched a programme once. It showed how the Russian Olympic team were trained to picture a movement, over and over, without stirring a limb. The brain perfected the action until it knew each pull of sinew, each tightening of ligament. Eventually, the brain could train the body to respond. The Russians swept up medals.

Miriam sweeps up her gold rings and puts them in her bag. They need to go for safekeeping. It says so on the paper that she's just signed.

A nurse busies herself in the room. She snaps a towel in line and straightens up a sheet.

'How are we today, Miriam?'

The nurse bandies first names as if she has known her patients from childhood.

'Not nervous are we?'

'Not at all,' Miriam answers. 'I'm looking forward to it. I've waited a long time for this day.'

'There's nothing to worry about. It's quite routine,' Nurse says, as if Miriam's words had floated out of the door without ever bumping against her ears.

Of course, Miriam could have said *No* at any point. She

could have refused to be here. Could have said: 'My body is my own and I'll do what I want with it.' But it's not often that life presents such an opportunity and Miriam believes in grabbing what comes at her with both hands. Lovers, travel, caviar and cocktails: she's enjoyed them all at different times of life.

'I'll get the doctor to have a word. He'll reassure you,' Nurse says. 'He's very good. Such careful hands. But after that it's up to you.'

'I have high hopes,' Miriam replies.

There's a clock on the wall. There are watches pinned to uniforms. The slow drip of a tap marks out the time.

'Has my daughter come?' Miriam asks. 'She's called Stella.'

'What a pretty name,' Nurse says and shakes her head.

Miriam closes her eyes and tries to picture her daughter striding along the corridor: a big woman, dutiful, a mother herself. She would surely do as she was asked?

The programme on gymnasts didn't go as far as this. Did the trainer ever sit motionless and will his young girls to leap and spin like feathers in the wind? Did his thoughts have any effect? If Miriam pictures her daughter's firm step and a bag in her hand, will it make her walk in?

'Stella?' she asks next time the nurse passes. Again, there's the shake of a head.

'She has to come. She promised. She's bringing me something.'

'You won't need anything until it's over. I'm sure she'll be here then.' Nurse lifts Miriam's wrist. 'I've to prep you,' she says.

'Not yet,' Miriam gasps.

In a battle of wills who would win?

But this part of 'prepping' turns out to be the process of getting Miriam washed and dressed in a gown with a slit at the back. It involves handing over her handbag and lifting the greyed curls that dip over her ears.

'No piercings? Good,' Nurse says.

Miriam sits on the edge of her bed. Her right hand is clutched in a fist. She's curtained off like an exhibit that shouldn't be seen. A cardigan encases her hips. It wraps round the back, to cover the slit. The cashmere is warm and soft against her sensitive skin. If Stella doesn't come soon it will change everything.

An orderly pops his head around the curtain.

'Are you decent?' he says. 'This was left for you at the desk. Your daughter will come back when it's over. I'll be taking you down in a minute.' He winks.

The brown paper bag holds a note from Stella:

I got what you asked for, Mum. And I put in soap and toothpaste just in case. The nurse says you aren't allowed flowers and you're fasting, so I gave her the grapes.

Miriam feels in the bag. Her fingers touch against paper and a box of rubber bands. She peers in. Yes! There's a hole puncher and a pen with indelible ink. She'd considered a biro, but is glad she went a step further than that in the end.

'Oh Stella! You're my girl,' she says.

There's a mirror in the bathroom. Would a cross, or a dot, be the best? Surgeons make mistakes the same as anyone else. She'd once had a friend who was fighting the first steps of anaesthetic oblivion, when she noticed the cross was drawn on the wrong breast. Just to make sure, Miriam draws two dots – large, round, blue – not to be missed. There's a hard surface to write against. It dampens the edge of the paper, but doesn't spread the ink. A drink would make her tongue less dry to lick. Her right hand slips down against her back, between the cardigan and the slit. The paper crinkles against her skin as she keeps her hand hidden and goes back to wait on the edge of her bed.

The anaesthetist is handsome in a young, flop-haired way. She smiles into his brown eyes and offers her left arm to be held in his firm grip. He does his job well. She doesn't hear the laughter or the discussion as they move her slack limbs.

'Are you going to do it?'

'Why not?' the surgeon says.

Somewhere a tap is dripping. Somewhere Miriam sleeps. Somewhere there is cutting and clamping. Somewhere something is stitched. Somewhere a liver is bleeding. Somewhere a man laughs out loud. And somewhere someone is twirling, round and back over the bars.

Miriam lifts one eyelid. It is heavy and the light is too bright. Nothing hurts. Not yet. But it will. She can imagine that all too well, but tries not to, just in case the thought makes the pain worse. Her mouth is drier than dry. And oh for the pour, the swirl, the sip and the smooth bite as liquid wets its way over her tongue and gums!

Nurse smoothes the hair back from Miriam's face.

'All over,' she says.

Or only just begun, Miriam thinks, before she slides back into sleep.

Stella's face is a picture, but she doesn't smile when she pulls back the curtain and stares at the bed.

'What do you think?' Miriam mumbles through lips that might crack for want of moisture. She gently manoeuvres her tongue.

'Why do you always have to make a show of yourself, Mum? Whatever possessed you? You've had half your liver removed for heaven's sake!'

'Open up my locker,' Miriam sighs. 'Get out the champagne. There are two glasses as well. One for you and one for me. I thought we could celebrate together. It's not every day I'm cleared out inside. An empty vessel that's me! And why this?' She waves a hand. 'Because every cloud has a silver lining,' she says.

'Mum! You can't have a drink!'

A torn envelope dangles from Miriam's wrist. A hole is punched in one corner and a rubber band holds it in place.

'Don't be silly, Stella! A small glass won't hurt.'

Nurse pops her head in the door with a smile: 'You got your wish. If I'd spotted it sooner I would have removed the note myself, but the doctor saw it. He said it had made his day.'

Miriam waits until the sound of soft shoes fades down the corridor. She holds up her wrist.

'You can read it,' she says. 'But in return you can pop that champagne.'

There's a battle at the back of Stella's eyes, but Miriam stares back: she's practiced and she knows which half will win.

Dear Doctor: I know you're about to take part of my liver away. You can have it. It served me well for a while and I've no one else to blame for the state it's in now. If you find anything else that's rotten inside me, then please take that out while you're at it. There's only one perfect thing ever came out of this body: that's my daughter, Stella, and she'll always be a star to me.

I'd just like to make a small request. I've never been brave enough to do it. I'm sure I would faint. So please pierce my ears while I can't feel a thing. To make it easy I've marked out the points and there are silver studs attached within.

A smile creeps over Stella's face. 'You're one of a kind,' she says.

Miriam reaches round for the bottle.

'You can't!' Stella hisses.

A towel softens the pop of the cork. The liquid pours like a gift. It froths and settles back down in the glass. Miriam twirls the stem in front of her face.

'Is it half full or half empty?' she asks.

'It could be either,' Stella sighs. She tilts her head and thinks again. 'But that's for most people. Not you. For you, it's whatever you decide you want it to be.'

Miriam closes her eyes and imagines her hand putting the frothing glass back on top of the locker. She pictures picking up the glass of iced water instead. A flutter of feather-like gymnasts rushes in to help her.

'This is a new me. A new start,' she says. 'I like the idea of long, dangly diamonds. And I like the idea of that nice young anaesthetist. But tell me honestly now, Stella, do you think, if I try hard enough, I can stay off the drink?'

The words lie between them. Miriam watches Stella and Stella looks back. The bubbles burst out of the untouched glass.

BLOOD RED

The sun is so low it shines in my eyes. Blood red. The fertile membrane of a part-hatched egg. It hangs on the horizon, sharing secrets that are best kept silent.

It's a strange thing, a red sun, you can look at it and your eyes don't hurt. There's no yellow flash burnt into your memory when you look away. It's like all the glitz and the glamour are gone and all that's left is the heavy, solemn reality. You can look underneath and see what should be seen. If you want to. If you care enough.

My mother is driving.

'Look at that sun,' she says. 'It's rolling down the side of the hill.'

I grip my seatbelt, half longing for collision. How could anything absorb so much blood and not burst?

I've always had a thing about bursting. My mother worries that I don't eat enough.

'You peck like a chicken,' she says. 'You'll end up like one too. All scrawny, running around on thin legs.'

She makes me drink milk. She always puts a glass on the table with my dinner.

'It's good for growing bones,' she says.

Too many bones! I think I can picture them growing. A bit like limescale on the inside of a kettle. A slow build up, little layer by little layer. Getting harder and harder, until you can't chip one with a fingernail. Then you can't chip it with a knife.

I think I stopped growing about a year ago. I'm small, but I don't think girls grow much once they are past thirteen. I tried explaining this to her. But then I started growing again and I didn't explain. I just drank the milk.

We have classes on 'health' in school. I think they're supposed to be about sex, but no one mentions the word. My mother had to sign a form. She laughed and looked away. 'Well I suppose there's no harm in you knowing,' she said. She seemed reassured by the rumour that we might be taught by a nun.

We only learned about 'things to eat' and 'not to take drugs'. We did something on 'abdominal exercises' and 'how good a friend should be'. We had to make lists. We never learned 'not to trust a cousin when he takes you into the shed'. We didn't find out that kisses from someone who knows how to kiss can make your legs go so wobbly and your brain so fluttery that your hands forget how to push away and your mouth can't take the breath to say no. By the time he starts to hurt you, it's too late. He's so many years older. He's so good looking. You'd feel such a fool. Your own shame keeps you silent.

My mother would only look away if I told her. She'd prefer not to know that someone else had touched me in a place she couldn't bring herself to name. She'd tell me the doorstep needed sweeping or my room was a mess. She puts her hands over her ears or sings when bad news comes on the radio. The twin towers are still standing in her head.

My best friend was Sharon Ann. I looked in my health book. There was a list of what a friend is and you had to tick yes and no in the boxes. I was pretty sure the answer was yes to 'someone you can trust' and 'someone who shares things with you'. I wasn't so sure about 'someone who always agrees with you'. I thought there might be a catch there. But it was really important that she agreed with me. If I told her, then she had to believe that it wasn't my fault. She had to believe that I didn't want to. She had to agree to hate him and not to tell anyone. I decided not to tell her until we had done that page in school. Then I could see how she answered the question. By the time we did the page, I'd already found out a lot about friends. Like, they laugh when they try to spook you by showing you the bloody layer round the inside of an egg that a hatching hen has kicked out of the nest. Like, they can prefer to go shopping with someone else because you never have money for new clothes anyway. Like, they talk about how fat you've got in whispers just loud enough to hear. Like, they ask you why you don't wear belly tops and have your navel pierced instead of slopping around in giant t-shirts they wouldn't even sleep in. A friend would notice. A friend would know.

Some people say that their mother is their best friend, but I know they are wrong. I'd been all the way down the Health Book list on mothers and I couldn't say yes to any of them. I really don't know if she 'thinks I'm great', or 'accepts me as I am'. She definitely didn't think I was great once I started to get fatter. Instead of calling me a chicken she called me a Christmas goose. She still put the milk on the table though and chattered about washing the kitchen curtains. There was no way I could talk to her about anything else. It's so easy to hide what people don't want to see.

Yesterday morning, instead of going to school, I went down to the shed at the bottom of the garden. I found an old piece of rag to stuff in my mouth. It tasted of machinery, cut grass and oil. My teeth bit through and I had to wad it again and wipe away the sweat when the pain wasn't so bad. My health book didn't say anything about this. 'How to travel on a bus', or 'the best way to do homework', was no use to me now. No one had told me of the agony it is possible to bear. How something starts as a small tightening and you just know it's going to get worse. Pain can spiral up and up until you think you must faint or die, because there's nothing else to do with such drowning. Everything hurts and you'll either squeeze to a mush or burst wide open. But then as suddenly, you are let go from the grip and you want to run. You want to escape before the same thing happens again. But you can't, because your belly drags down and that's where the pain is, right in the centre of yourself.

I know I screamed. I couldn't help it. A wild animal scream that frightened me. There was wetness and blood and I slipped and rolled, not caring, not wanting to live.

Once he came out it wasn't so bad.

I looked at him on the floor of the shed. He was grey, with bits of dry earth and leaves sticking in among the white and the red. His lips were bright. They slumped down in a sad berry line. His eyes were shut. How had something so big come out of me?

I paid a lot of attention. I looked at every bit. I wanted him to know I had taken notice – that I had found out who he was. I wanted him to know that if he made a sound I would listen, that he could tell me anything and I would trust him. That I would help if he needed me. I heaved out every last bit of gristle and flesh, of stringy cord, to follow him. I hugged him tight and told him that whatever he did, I would always love him. He never made a sound. His eyes didn't open. His skin was grey.

The ground was soft behind the roses and easy to dig. I made a small hole and laid him in. I didn't know what else to do. I'd never been taught about birth and death.

I wondered how many babies lay buried among roses. I wondered how many of my friends had grown fat and then thin. All over this land there could be small bones softening into unconsecrated earth. While teachers argued over who would teach health, my baby's flesh would rot down, his blood would seep to grow bright red blooms. And no one would know except me.

But then this morning I learned that nothing is ever so simple. It was on the news on the radio, although I could hardly hear above my mother's singing. There was the voice of the priest, the head teacher, a neighbour, all giving their opinions. They were horrified, disgusted. I could tell from the way they answered the questions. I could tell from the way they gave little coughs before speaking.

A dog had been seen carrying a small body. It had dug it up. Covered in earth. A boy. The child had never breathed.

A stillbirth. The mother should come forward. Seek medical attention.

My mother turned the radio off and sang louder. I walked to the rose bed and scuffed the earth flat with my shoe. My sin, my son, had risen to the surface and been stolen away. I should have dug deeper.

I wore my biggest jumper. I hunched forward under the weight of my school bag.

'Did you hear the news?' Sharon Ann asked. She was too excited to forget that I had been dropped as a friend. 'I wonder if it chewed it. Yuck, it could have eaten an arm right off.'

A sickening pain griped in my belly and a gush of warm liquid seeped between my legs. I sat in the toilet through Geography. I couldn't bear to move. Leaking blood onto wadded tissue, while tears refused to flow. At first break, I came out to eat my chocolate bar in a corner.

'It's one of the New Age Travellers down by the river,' Sharon Ann said. 'It was one of their dogs.'

'Do you think the person will be put in prison?' I asked. I had to. Sharon Ann was no expert, but who else would know the answer?

'My mam says they'll be put in the mental hospital. There must be something wrong with their mind. It's probably the drugs. They're all addicts, you know. Their children will probably be taken away and put into care.'

I needed to sit down.

Who would know? How could anyone be sure? Were there permanent scars that said 'this one has had a stillborn child'? If the bleeding would only stop, then there would be nothing left to betray me.

I remembered once, as a small child in infant class, my teacher threatened to lift everyone's skirt and check our knickers. Someone had wet themselves during the school photo and no one was owning up. I hadn't done it, but my pants were damp. I asked my friend Mary, who sat next to me and she said hers were the same. We lived that day in terror, until someone confessed. Since then, I've always half believed that a teacher can inspect underwear at will. Just let them try now. I'd tell them I've got the monthly curse if they do.

I was told off twice for not listening in Maths. I thought I might throw up in History. I went to the secretary and asked them to phone home.

'There's a stomach bug going around,' the secretary said. She let me sit in her office until I saw my mother's red car roll into the car park.

'You aren't too bad are you?' my mother asked. 'You can sit in the car while I do my shopping?'

I knew then I'd be home late. Later than the school bus would have reached our gate, but at least I'd only have my mother for company. She would never talk about dogs and children playing by the river with matted hair and no clothes. She would talk about the new saucepan she got in Murphy's, or how hard it was to buy wooden clothes-pegs these days. I lay on the back seat and let her words wash over me. She complained a little at having to put her shopping in the front. When she brought her good black suit from the cleaners I offered to move to the front seat so it wouldn't get crumpled.

We passed Miss O'Sullivan's garden. The flowers were enormous. There were reds and whites, yellows and pale pinks.

'Just look at those roses,' my mother said.

That made me think. Would our roses have grown bigger? Would roots have twined around limbs and in at that sad berry mouth? Perhaps now, the priest, the teacher, the neighbour will bury him in a small white box, where roots cannot reach.

The red sun is round as a belly. There is red in my eyes. There is red seeping through my clothes and staining the car seat.

'Look it's rolling again. Look at it rolling down the hill like a big red ball,' my mother says.

Soon the sun will collide with us. Soon it will roll us up into that soft red warmth.

'Oh look,' my mother says as I step from the car. 'The butcher never wraps things well enough. The beef heart has leaked all over the seat and it's stained the back of your school skirt too.'

She looks into my eyes and I don't look away. I need her to see whose heart is really bleeding. For a moment I see a thought flicker at the back of her eyes. Or maybe it's only the reflection of a blood red sun. She puts an arm around my waist and her hand touches the soft flesh of my belly.

'It'll be alright,' she says. 'Even blood will clean up nicely. No one will ever know.'

'I will,' I whisper.

My mother starts to hum: 'Bring me sunshine ...'

CRYING FOR WORMS

A butterfly lands upon a flower. Its wings of gold and red tremble against the blue petals. They look damp, new minted, a first fresh fluttering in the warm morning air. The cat jumps cleanly and swallows once or twice as it returns to the ground. I wonder if the butterfly wriggles and jiggles and tickles inside her, but that was an old woman and a spider, I'm sure.

The cat settles on a sun-soaked cushion of aubretia on the garden wall. I return to my deckchair and wait, unsure what might happen on such a day.

When I was very young I had a hiding place in the middle of a large rhododendron bush. I knew that nothing could touch me there. The earth was always dry. The shiny leaves didn't fall and leave me exposed. I planted an apple pip and an orange seed down among the twining roots, but they didn't grow. So I scooped a hole and nestled a full-fleshed Golden Delicious in it, with skin unblemished and stem pointing upward. I carried water in a plastic cup, while dreaming of a small tree full of pale green fruit. I imagined the grit of dry earth rubbing into my bare legs as I sat and chewed through my own sweet apples in my own safe place.

After two weeks of waiting, I dug the apple up. The flesh was brown and soft, woven with the tracks of small creatures. Millipedes and woodlice had eaten their fill, but I was too young to understand the complexities of intertwining layers of life. I threw the apple over a wall and firmed the earth flat again with the sole of my best red sandal. I carried a small milking stool into my hiding place. I no longer trusted the bare earth not to turn my skin to a rotten pulp.

Many years later I took a boyfriend behind the glossy foliage in order to explore his mouth with mine, out of sight of the blank house windows. I felt the stool collapse and press its rotten legs into my back as the boy's legs sought to entrap mine. I knew I had gone too far, that I no longer had any secret place; that a rotten apple and a rotten stool had tried to warn me. But I also knew for sure that no seeds could grow there.

I wasn't a disobedient child, just a dreamer. I did collect the eggs, but I often forgot where I'd left them. Perhaps I just wanted to retrace the special moments of each day: to revisit the fox's footprints in the soft mud by the stream; to see if the dawn webs still sparkled in the afternoon furze.

It wasn't that I forgot my mother's warnings. I knew, as I

touched the oiled blade of a hanging scythe, that it was sharp. When a bright red line stroked across my thumb, I was mildly surprised. It didn't hurt. I wrapped it round and round, in a piece of cotton torn from the frayed edge of my knickers, until no more red seeped through, then I went to see if the swallows had returned to the eaves of the small shed.

When my thumb began to throb with each heartbeat and the skin stretched red and hot to the touch, I showed it to my mother. First she blamed herself for not noticing sooner. Then she blamed me for ignoring her warnings. A lock was fixed to the small shed and that year I missed the sight of new-hatched swallows open-ing their greedy mouths. I had to content myself with the flight of the parents going in and out through a hole under the eaves. They carried small wriggling offerings. No matter how much they brought, I could still hear baby voices calling for more. To ease their job I collected worms from under stones and laid them out on a wall close by. Sometimes I tried beetles, but they ran away too fast. At the end of August the swallows all flew away.

Mother did warn me about boys: 'They are all after one thing,' she said. 'And once you've given them that, they only want more. If you start saying "no" after you've once said "yes" then they lose all interest. Listen to me girl and never say "yes" in the first place. It's the safest way.'

I didn't know what she was talking about, but she had a sad look in her eyes. It seemed best not to ask for a repeat. Anyway, I'd probably not heard the important bit, because I was watching a spider guarding its egg sack high on the wall. For a while after that, I always said 'no' when a boy offered me anything.

My life has been littered with unconnected events. It's only now – when I have the time to watch butterflies and think that life can be as short as the unfolding of a painted wing, or as long as the slow and certain flow of continuous life from big bang to final apocalypse – that I begin to tease out the links.

At sixteen, my mother got me a job in the village shop. She put on her good coat and hat and went in to buy a newspaper. There had been long discussions the night before as to what the best purchase would be. We had milk of our own and Mother had always baked her own bread. Toiletries looked frivolous and no one would be seen buying potatoes before mid-spring, when the home supply could decently have run out. We always bought ham in town, since that sold in the village was rotten.

A newspaper set the right tone. I had an education and my father liked to know what was happening in the world, so the paper wouldn't go to waste.

My mother's back was as straight and her shoulders as square as if she'd hidden a broom in the back of her coat. She marched into the shop, leaving me outside by the sacks of swedes and bundles of firewood.

For a week I believed that she had forced them to hire me. I worked in a half apologetic way, always willing to do any task, always trying to compensate for my mother's bullying. I made a special effort to sell more ham than usual and never to look smug when a farmer bought milk. I eventually found out that I had been the only applicant for the job, but the tone had been set: I worked in a state of apology for the next three years.

The hayshed was large and open on three sides. It was my job to make sure the cattle had their fill in the winter. I carried armfuls of sweet hay, smelling of summer days and harvest home. The seeds stuck to my green jumper, but it was old and I only wore it around the farm.

I went to the hay barn in the dark of a winter evening. I was wearing my best skirt and a short red jacket. Clammy to my touch was the hand of a travelling salesman from up the country. I wouldn't stack shelves for the rest of my life. I needed to fly. A travelling life seemed so romantic.

I'd felt pity for his long thin neck, his loose grey suit as he'd leaned across the shop counter. Like the heron alone at the edge of the pond: fishing, fishing for what he could get.

A spider must have spun a web between the pillars of the barn. I pushed through it as I left. The silky fibres stroked across my face. My heron flew slowly, laboriously away. He must have had other pools to fish.

I crept silently up the stairs, hearing the creak on the turn, hearing the snores of my mother's deep sleep, feeling foolishly free. There were hayseeds in the seams of my red jacket. There were seeds itching in the waistband of my best skirt. Fine filaments of silver thread clung to my belly. How could a body be immune in the presence of so much fecundity?

My mother wore her good coat and hat to wave me off on the Dublin train, but she forgot the broom: her back was bent and her shoulders sagged down.

I once heard a fairy story about a little man who killed seven flies at one blow. He made a belt that proclaimed he killed 'seven at a blow' and so everyone was afraid of him. I don't remember how the story ended, but I was amazed that anyone could believe such a thing.

I was hasty in my judgement. Life has taught me how easy it

is to hide a truth and to create a lie. Self-deception is the hardest bit, once that's achieved, everyone else just falls into line.

If we can only interpret the signs, we know what to expect. A cat eats a butterfly. I lie in the sun and scratch an itch on my arm. A million spiders spin a million webs and where some catch flies, others lay traps for pregnant girls.

After eighteen years I expected to hear a knock on the door. It never came, but that was the one weak moment when I might have told. I might have picked up a phone and said about the sickness in the room in Dublin, about throwing up all the way across the Irish sea. I might have confessed that living in England wasn't about better jobs or looser living. It was about secrets, sickness and fear. About giving birth to a tiny daughter all covered in red and white. It was the relief of handing her over into other hands and the guilt forever at having done so.

The knock never came. The phone never rang. I never had to confess to a caring husband. I never had to tell a much-loved son that he wasn't the first.

I would like to watch the cat all day. To pretend that the 'nevers' are still unbroken. I would like to watch a nest of swallows hatch under the eaves and feel that another spring has passed and nothing will change. But daydreams are for children.

High above, two planes leave vapour trails in the blue sky. To my earthbound eyes, they are crossed paths, a point at which breath can mingle and form a perfect drop from two sighs. I know in reality there is a gulf between them: that a passenger on one, sipping her drink and reading her paper, will have no idea of the other plane or the cross they leave as a pledge in the sky.

Why did she wait until she was thirty before tracking me down?

It wasn't the rhododendron place, or the haybarn, that betrayed me. It wasn't the acid earth that favoured a girl. It wasn't lying down rather than standing up. It wasn't even his insistence that the cut off finger of a plastic glove was 'just as good'. It was my fault I dreamed through the 'yesses' and 'noes'. It was my fault I yearned for swallows flying away, for a bright unfurling of wings in flight on a warm summer day.

'Just a minute Mam,' I said before we left for the station. I ran down the damp path to the ducks at the pond. The small brown females riffled their beaks through the water. The colourful male stuck his chest forward and watched with a sharp little eye.

I threw stones in the water and shouted. I flapped the arms of my grey coat and called in a voice that might resemble an eagle. I leapt my high heels up off the mud and splattered down with a splash up the back of my stockings. They didn't fly. They just huddled and grumbled at the far end of the pond: content with too small a world. I just needed to check I was doing the right thing.

The doorbell rings. High and shrill it startles me, although I have been waiting. I move heavy legs to bear my weight and use willpower to steer a course. Up the back steps from the patch of green lawn to the kitchen door. Through the small bright room where sunlight shines from white appliances. An empty house waiting, while she waits on the other side of the door. I can't turn the handle. I have lost the lithe body that let me run after ducks. I have lost the freedom of thought that set me certain, unflinching on a course.

'What do you want to be when you grow up?' my mother had asked when I was small. Her eyebrows rose up, nearly to touch her curly brown hair. Her eyes were waiting for words such as hairdresser, teacher or Mammy, sparkling with expectation.

'A bird,' I said.

She flapped her hands against her apron and laughed. 'What sort of bird?' she asked.

'One that flies away. Like a swallow. Not a chicken. Not a duck. I want to be one that flies far away. But I'll never make a nest,' I said.

'You're a strange one,' my mother said. 'Won't you be sad to leave home?'

'But I'll come back each year for a visit,' I said. 'I'll live in the bush at the bottom of the garden.'

My mother shook her head and looked sad.

I will turn the handle in a moment. I will look into eyes that might be as blue as my own. I want to know what to say first. I want to get the links all sorted, to sift the important from everything else. Rotten apples; flying birds; cut thumbs; a broom for courage; a homely brown duck that never left the pond; a spider measuring the imperceptible swell of a fertile belly; hayseed against the red seam of a jacket; a butterfly given no more chance than a flutter at life; possibilities ended before they're begun; beginnings possible, without an end. Will I be pinned beneath a paw or swallowed whole?

When the words are sorted I will open the door. I will

explain to the hand that is pressing the bell: to the fearful, or hopeful, face. I will try to turn any anger aside.

'I was too young, too innocent. I had travelled nowhere and was afraid of being trapped. I was scared of the hard work, the continual demands. I could scarcely look after myself. I was afraid I would daydream, while you cried for worms.'

LIGHT, THOUGHT
AND EVELYN

In the beginning there was a 'bang'. It was an extremely large 'bang': one that would have been frightening, if fright had been a possibility. Perhaps the noise was caused by atoms crashing together in a primordial soup. Or perhaps an omnipotent God roared out and declared that all was good. Whatever the cause and whatever the timescale – a week or billions of years – light somehow managed to spread through the darkness and life's possibilities were released.

'What was that noise?' Evelyn asked, of no one in particular: probably because there was no one around to be particular about. It wasn't that Evelyn was choosy about her friends. It was simply that she was the only person alive as yet and so had to address her remarks into the people-less swill that washed all around. Her mouth flopped open and her tongue licked over her teeth while she searched for words. Circumstances had rather rapidly overtaken her, leaving little to comment on other than the startling noise.

'The weather could be better,' she muttered, peering into the swirling grey mists. Immediately, a drift of blue appeared with a small white cloud floating at its centre.

'Enough for a sailor's trousers,' she said, although sailors were still billions of years from being conceived. A wet slap of brine caught in her nostrils and a garment with a leg's length of side-piping came through the mist and as rapidly went. A string of something like grey spaghetti drifted past her head. A blob, with the texture of leftover sauce, clung to her knee.

'Well,' she said. 'That's odd. There's no other word for it.'

Off to one side of her ear, a string of protein coiled and wrapped to spell words like *strange*, *peculiar*, *freakish* and *bizarre*. There was even the start of what might have been *idiosyncratic* and the potential for the earth's first thesaurus, but spelling was never Evelyn's strong point. She didn't even notice the tumble of possibilities as they snaked at the back of her head and were sucked off into the gloom.

In ordinary circumstances, Evelyn didn't miss much. She was good at noticing what needed to be done, who needed attention and who would benefit from an extra smile. She just wasn't used to floating, suspended at the beginning of time. And, on top of that, her back ached. The back was a new thing! Usually she suffered from throbbing feet, or a head that stabbed with the noise of too many customers demanding service all at once.

'Come to think of it,' she said. 'Where are all the tables and chairs? They must be here somewhere?'

As she spoke, so it was. A row of neat red Formica tops appeared, followed rapidly by matching plastic chairs that drifted just in front of her face.

'Now stop that,' she said. 'How can I wipe you clean if you don't stay fixed to the floor? Stop floating this minute!'

As she spoke, so it was. A world coalesced around her in shades of blue and grey tiling. Mountains were overlooked and forests too, in favour of a patch of black and white checked linoleum. Evelyn alighted onto the café floor, followed by the tables and chairs.

'At least now I can sit down.' She stretched to ease her back. 'And there are no customers that need attention. I wouldn't mind a coffee though.'

As she spoke, so it was. A blue and white striped mug materialised on the tabletop. The murky brown liquid sent a swirl of steam up Evelyn's nose. She opened her mouth to speak again, but a matching sugar bowl and milk jug appeared before she could do so.

'Very nice, thank you,' she said.

Not confident enough yet to demand a teaspoon, Evelyn blew at her coffee and tried to dissolve the sugar by swirling the liquid around until it almost lapped over the edge of the cup.

Within the light there was thought. And from this thought were born all things. Time had no meaning as yet, so a day could encompass a million years. Life could grow and multiply with no restriction. The only limits were the concepts that thought could form.

After the coffee, there were other things wished, or spoken, into being. Soon, Evelyn's little corner of the universe was filled with useful items, such as a television set, a microwave, three different women's magazines and an assortment of comfortable slippers. The television set suffered badly from static and Evelyn had not yet decided on her favourite instant meal. A small microbe, still to be named salmonella, was the first living thing that she created. And it was not good.

'I'll not eat that!'

She threw the mess into a bin, where it could fester until the first refuse collection would be thought of – or perhaps a hedge to toss a plastic bag behind.

'I wouldn't mind a game of bingo!' Evelyn clapped her hands. Instantly the world leapt through aeons of evolution, to give birth to a crowded hall where a young man shouted 'legs eleven' and a woman screamed 'house'. There was even the smell of sweat, perfume, cigarette smoke, stained underwear and pheromones: all distilled into a perfect racy blend. Most of the people were fifty, or older, but the girl who handed out the prizes still had voluptuous curves and the young man who called the numbers didn't think of two fat ladies when he saw eighty-eight. It seemed that mankind's continued existence was assured.

'It's like being my own fairy godmother,' Evelyn gasped. 'It's even better than winning the Lottery!'

In an ecstasy of creation, she called for: fish and chip shops, free clothes for women, better hairstylists and more old-fashioned films at the cinema.

'Drinks are on me!' She waved her arms in wide circles, while demanding a replica of her favourite bar in one corner.

'Keep your hands to yourself,' she said to the elderly man sitting next to her. He smiled and looked into his drink.

'Now, if you were forty years younger, it would be different,' she added, with a glint in her eye. Evelyn lifted the hand of the muscular young man back onto her knee.

The beasts that walk on four legs, the birds of the air, the fish of the sea, the fruit of the land, were not thought of and so did not exist: except perhaps as dipped in batter or sliced into chips.

'I want a servant, a big house, a four-poster bed!'

The bingo players demanded some tea. With a wave of her hand Evelyn was about to produce a banquet, but a loud clanging sound burst around her head. Her eyes flicked open. Not God after all, she realised with a pang of regret. Pity, she thought, as she slammed her fist down on the alarm clock and tucked her head under the pillow, trying to regain the feeling of omnipotence.

All manner of living things came to exist in the world. Life flowed through cycles where each form had its place. And with thought came mankind's wonder at all that was, and all that might have been.

The dream unsettled Evelyn for the rest of the day.

Her mind was not on her work and the boss shouted at her more than once.

'What's got into you?' he asked. 'You're daydreaming all the time. I don't pay for lazy Mondays.'

'There are a lot of problems in the world,' Evelyn replied.

'Yeah, like table number two,' he said, wagging a finger in front of her face.

'There's more to life than that,' she muttered, as she delivered the burgers and chips.

After work, Evelyn wandered aimlessly for a while, noticing the beauty of the tall buildings that lined a particular street. The fine bold red of a sunset sky held her captive for a quarter of an hour on the way home. She'd never before noticed the

Joyce Russell

shape of fine-fingered leaves. She bought two lottery tickets, hoping that some divine inspiration might guide her choice, but she didn't even match one number.

'Stupid mattress,' she complained, as she tried to get comfortable in bed. 'It's got more lumps than I have. How can anyone expect a decent night's sleep!'

That night, she dreamed of her mother. The old woman spread to fill a seat by the fire. Her hands plucked at the fabric stretched tight across her knee.

'Getting above yourself aren't you!' the puckered mouth said. 'You never had enough brains to see that you were the slowest one in the class. There's nothing but fresh air up between those fine big ears. Accept it girl! I wouldn't want to live in any world you dreamed up!'

'Well you wouldn't have to. You're dead.'

'But not forgotten.'

Her mother melted before her eyes, but the words still spun as they had spun for years: not enough brains, big ears, accept it!

Light and thought became a part of the cycle of life. They fed the living earth and nourished mankind. But some dark thoughts – pale things that needed no light or inspiration – festered in their secret way. Hope could not flourish when light and thought were withdrawn.

'I'm depressed,' Evelyn said to her doctor on Tuesday. 'I dreamed that I was God and all I did was re-create the little things of my life. I had a chance to build a world and I made a bingo hall. I was too stupid to do any better than that.'

The doctor scribbled a note on her file and prescribed a drug to help her cope.

'Perhaps you should see a specialist,' he suggested.

'Are there specialists in disempowered gods?' she asked.

That night, Evelyn went to bingo. She gazed fondly at the old man on her left, remembering the firm grasp of a younger hand. He pushed a lower set of dentures forward with his tongue then sucked them back. She wondered if he lamented the loss of his youth.

There was a large loudspeaker and a stack of chairs in the corner where her bar had appeared. How many people would really leap to their feet if she offered free drinks and how many more would tell her to shush while they listened for numbers, or just ask for two sugars and a splash of milk?

Evelyn didn't notice when her card was filled. It didn't matter that she could have won a box of biscuits and had the thrill of shouting 'house' to the crowded hall.

'Do you ever wish that your life had been different?' Evelyn asked the old man.

'How do you mean?' he said. His eyes didn't lift.

'Well, just that it hadn't all led here, to a point where bingo is the highlight of the week?'

He chanced a quick look sideways before rechecking his card. 'There's nothing wrong with this,' he said.

'Perhaps not,' she replied, 'but I don't even know about other things. I know the streets around here, and the people in them, as if they are the beginning and end of the world. But they aren't you know, or at least they shouldn't be.'

'I wouldn't want to go away from here at my age. This is good enough for me.' His face brightened. 'You could go on a cruise! I know someone who did that. It was the best thing ever, they said.' His teeth popped forward and back with the thought. 'They never went on another one, but still you could give it a try.'

'I don't much like floating, but I think I might get a cat,' she said.

'I like cats.' The teeth sucked out and in. 'They don't question their lives. They're content with what they've got.'

Evelyn opened a drawer when she got home. She pulled out a clean sheet of paper and wrote 'Cats' at the top. She turned the picture of her mother face down on the sideboard.

From thought was born the concept of power. And some souls were born to greatness and some to toil upon the face of the earth in obscurity. But all hopes could wander in a dream and events could still conspire to alter destiny.

The church door groaned, announcing her entrance, as Evelyn slipped in for the Wednesday service. She bobbed her head and dipped into a pew at the back. The seat was hard beneath her and her knees almost touched the one in front. The sermon was all about forgiveness and redemption, how it was never too late to make a fresh start. A choir sang. High, sweet voices mingled with low ones and both twisted together in the sparkles of dust before the stained glass.

Evelyn went home and wrote 'Music' on her sheet of paper. She now had two words to think about.

That night, Evelyn dreamed that she was shooting her mother.

'I'm sorry,' she said, before she pulled the trigger. 'It's just got to be done. If you're dead anyway, then this shouldn't hurt.' She woke without hearing if the old woman made a reply.

And each strived to reach perfection and to create perfection in all that surrounded them. But the human mind was limited and could not conceive a world in its entire and diverse form.

On Thursday, for the first time in her life, Evelyn walked up the grey steps of the museum. She moved slowly from exhibit to exhibit. Her mind raced as she stared at fossils, bones and tools from the past. On the way home, she bought a magazine with a picture of a rainforest on the front and a child with piercing eyes on an inner page. She studied each photograph and read all the captions, progressing steadily from cover to cover. She took out her list and balanced the pen against her lip. 'Equality', she wrote at last, and then 'Love'. She thought a while before adding 'Trees' and 'Mushrooms'.

Evelyn dreamed that she was making a speech. A crowd stood around her and she wanted them to listen, but everyone talked too loudly. She shouted at the top of her voice. It was important for her to tell them that there were things of beauty in the world, things that should not be forgotten.

'All things are created equal,' she roared. The crowd laughed and applauded as if she had cracked a good joke.

The list grew. Evelyn bought books on geography and wild-life. On Friday a man fixed a satellite dish to the house, so she could watch programmes on history and the natural world. The woman at the flower shop told her the names of all the blooms. Evelyn wrote them down so she could be sure that the right name always fitted with the right flower. She watched the way the river moved, discovered about the life of an eel and of things that live in the deepest parts of the ocean. Her list grew boldly in black ink.

She wrote down foods that she liked and, in the interest of diversity, sampled ugli fruit, yams and mangoes from the supermarket. The higher levels of the earth's atmosphere were beyond her understanding, but she listed 'a starry night' and 'the full moon'.

All week long, she served lunchtime sausages, chips and chicken nuggets to customers who were unaware of her quest. Every afternoon, she scoured the shelves of the library for new and interesting facts.

For each beginning was a new hope. Each act of creation brought forth new ways of seeing the world. And she looked upon her work and knew that it was good.

Evelyn was tired by Saturday night. She promised herself a good day's rest on the Sunday. Maybe she'd find an old film on the satellite channels and put her feet up on the settee. And if things went well, then maybe she'd spare a moment or two to consider all that she'd achieved in the previous week.

'I'm not stupid,' she said, to the back of a face-down photograph. 'There's a lot more in my head than fresh air. I've read lots of books. I've learned lots of things. It's not too late. I've started to work out who I am and who I might want to be.'

A brochure for cruises lay on the counter. An ad for kittens was stuck with a magnet against the door of the fridge. A cup of warm milk and honey lay in her stomach like a comfort. She washed her face and brushed her teeth. The street was lit with yellow lamps and the rain made light scatter in golden stars behind the closed curtain. A siren wailed off into the distance, taking someone's calamity on to the next stage.

'I'm ready,' Evelyn declared at last, lying rigid upon her mattress. 'Just give me one more chance. I've got it all here now.'

She tapped at the front of her nightdress with the tip of her finger and pressed the sheets of paper down against her skin.

And the world slept with Evelyn, unaware of the deity within: unaware of the new beginnings that she might dream.

LEAST SAID

They carried her body on a door. One hand trailed down to brush the cloudy tops of bog cotton. Myrtle rose like incense where she passed. One man to each corner. Eight boots soaked with dew. Eight eyes locked open, windblown and wetted, searching the edge of the moor. Far on and beyond the horizon there are black sucking pools. There are places where heather makes a matting of purple. There are places where a mother can be lost and a father too.

My grandmother said that five people went out in the morning mist and three were drawn back with the night. She stroked my hair: 'Don't you remember? You held my hand. You waved bye bye.'

In my mind, my mother wore white. Her hair spilled out to either side. She was posing for a painting: something Pre-Raphaelite. I've studied those paintings and listened to cushioned footfalls. In fact, I'm sitting in front of my favourite one now. My ears are attuned to hushed whispers, to breath sucked back and blown out in a silent moment of awe.

People stand back to admire. I reach out a hand to touch, but it falls far short. The attendant is watching. She knows well enough how I am compelled to reach forward, how just one tip of a finger can scratch back a flake.

'It's personal. I need to know what lives in the oil and the brushstroke. I need to know what ghosts hide beneath the paint!'

That's what I answered when the attendant asked last week what I thought I was doing. As she led me to the door, I apologised. I read her name on an embossed badge. I used it three times. That didn't stop her showing me the door, but her hand was gentle when it brushed my elbow with a feather touch. She lets me back in from time to time, but always stands close by.

I sit and stare. If looks could scratch at a painting, the Lady of Shalott would be worn down to a first wash of colour and there would be bare canvas instead of her hands and her eyes.

The secrets are always underneath. A scratch is sometimes the only way to tell: no matter if it raises blood, or peels back a flake, or exposes lies.

I listened to what my grandmother said. I know that five went out and three came back. I waved a hand, but over the years I added to that: the body rocked as the men knelt and then rose. Their arms trembled with the weight. My mother had hair as brown as a ripe nut. She had skin that loved the sun. Her eyes were blue I decided, or black. How I wished that it was her at my side, holding my fist balled up in her own, while four men lifted a door at each corner and a different hand, perhaps one from a picture, stirred the scent of myrtle like incense.

My grandmother coloured my life. She raised me from an open-eyed child, stare-struck with fright, to an adult that tries to have x-ray eyes. No small feat on her part.

We lived together on the high moor in a house that backed towards the wind: although the wind was treacherous and knew how to beat on all sides. A thousand sheep walked the moor and maybe another thousand lambs each spring, but each face seemed a familiar friend when I went out to play. Some had curls near the ears and one had a patch of black, like a pirate, right over its eye. I can bleat with forty different voices, but if I try to show off my talent, the attendant would surely draw a line.

The Lady of Shalott isn't much older than me. She lets her quilt drag in the water and why does she need candles when it's broad daylight? The longer I stare, the more I see. This painting isn't about my mother, this painting is me: I'm adrift and floating since Grandmother died.

Are old people always wise? When I was sick, Grandmother knew to stir raw eggs into honey. She'd splash a drop of brandy on top. I drank it down once and was never sick again, or at least I learned how to swallow down the bile and not to confess if my stomach pained.

'Least said, soonest mended,' was her favourite way of expressing things.

She didn't say much about five people and three. She didn't say more about trailing hands and what colour a dress might have been. She'd said enough in her opinion. If I didn't mend after that, well I'd only myself to blame.

I was given a bike when I was old enough. Grandmother had pains in her knees and her sight was dim. If I wanted any schooling it was the only way. I rode the bike, then caught the bus; Grandmother had the timing down to four minutes of error each trip. She nodded and smiled when people praised her for raising a child at her stage in life, but her lips were tight over her teeth and she didn't answer the questions that slid into the conversation sideways.

She whispered in my ear at night: 'If you're smart, you'll hold your tongue. Loose words waste breath.'

Some things were taboo. The numbers five and three weren't spoken aloud even when, for homework, I had to count up to a hundred and back down again. When I practised the times tables I had to stand out on the moor and entertain the sheep.

I always did like to draw. Give me a pencil and paper and I could be quiet for a day. Of course, there were taboos again. No pictures could contain more than two people: upright and preferably Grandmother and me. She dressed me in kilts with straps over the shoulders and a big safety pin. The wool was hard wearing in her opinion, but I always made holes in grey tights at the knees. My hair was cut short and the cows-lick was held down with a hairgrip. I complained that no one else went to school dressed that way.

'Well it takes all sorts,' my grandmother said.

Boiled mutton. Bread pudding. Cabbage that was soft enough to chew without sticking between her teeth. A chamber pot with a blue flower and a ring like rime on the inside. A high bed with a hard pillow, a feather cover and a squeak that lived in the springs. If I screamed with fear in the night, she would come and slip into bed beside me and speak out a list.

'We must be thankful for what we've got, and at least we have one another,' she said.

I added the bit about the teeth and the squeak. I added the 'ring like rime': the words were pleasing to me. When she fell asleep, Grandmother counted in her dreams. Sometimes a five or a three whistled from the gap where her teeth should have been.

She didn't think it was healthy for an old woman to sleep next to a young girl: 'The old will sap the strength from the young,' she sighed. But she liked to hold me in her arms and whisper that I was her dear, sweet child.

Of course people asked: 'Where's your mummy?' They didn't mention a daddy, but there were other people in my class without one of those, so it wasn't so strange.

'I don't understand.' The lady behind the post-office counter had a puzzled look on her face. I held out my hand for a stamp. I took my change. My fingers curled round and I turned away.

'How exactly are you related to Miss Browne?' She didn't emphasise the e at the end, although she knew it was there: she saw Grandmother's mail come in with the name spelled that way.

If I look at a picture for long enough, and especially a big canvas, I feel myself fall in. There doesn't have to be water, trees will do, but sometimes they fall outward and land on me. When I turn pale and close my eyes, the attendant steps forward. She asks in a gentle voice if I'd like a sip of water, if I'm all right. She doesn't offer a handkerchief, but the tears are inside so she wouldn't see the need.

'If five went out and three came back ...' I asked before my grandmother passed away. She winced when I mentioned the numbers, but she was in pain all the time at that stage, '… what happened to my father?'

'Love,' she answered back. 'He loved her, but they both loved their child. Oh that's enough explaining. Go talk to the sheep!'

It wasn't until her breath paused and picked up again, that she gave me something more than a door, a hand and the high church of incense blowing around the moor.

'Just like a fairy tale,' she rasped.

Her mouth bit back with the tightest of smiles.

The Lady of Shalott has stepped straight off those pages. She could be a princess searching for a frog, or a beautiful beggar girl about to find her handsome prince.

'Is it really a fairy tale, or are unhappy endings waiting just beyond the frame?'

I speak aloud and the attendant wags a long pale finger. There's a flash of red at the end and curled over her palm are a row of painted tips. I shake my head in return. I'm not about to misbehave. She looks around and keeps her voice low: 'The Lady of Shalott was under an enchantment. She could never see the world as it really was. Only as a reflection. But she chose to look out at the real world in the end.'

'Did she survive once she'd looked?' I have to ask.

'No.' The attendant turns a shiny heel against the floor. 'She's dying as she floats in the boat. I suppose she couldn't bear the isolation any more. Better to be free, than live under a curse.'

Sixteen years of a door and more have led to this point. I want to say: 'Are you sure?'

There was nothing to halt our passage from room to room in my grandmother's house. There were places chiselled out and painted over in the frames, but the doors had gone before I can recall. My grandmother didn't explain.

'Out with the old and in with the new,' was all she said.

The new was the two of us. We were contained, but the rooms ran into one another like an art gallery and we were the paintings jumped down off the walls. The wind found its way in. It blew along corridors and touched fingers over a sleeping face. A thousand bleats in the night talked just to me.

I heard her die. I was downstairs warming the teapot and spooning the leaves. I'd paused for longer than I should: dreaming of tales that couldn't possibly be. There was nothing to stop her last breath floating down the stairs. I'd swear she tried to call my name. I dropped the tea and the milk as well. Sugar cubes rolled all over the floor. Her eyes were closed and her mouth was open. I could imagine, 'It comes to us all in the end', but her tongue was as blue as a stillborn lamb's and couldn't shape the words.

They wouldn't let me bury her in a winding sheet. They insisted on oak or mahogany. With wood all around her, encased, Grandmother couldn't stay silent. It was only a matter of time before she escaped.

In my dreams, she knocked on the closed front door. She peered in at the window and wailed. She floated like a helium-filled sheep across the moor, lifted up on the wind in a shroud. Her hands were too high to stir up any incense, but she tickled the clouds and stirred up a storm instead.

I had plans. I had less insidious dreams. I would sell the house if I had to. I could go to Art College. How young I was then! Six months to this point have seen me grow older, but wiser is a painful thing.

'Old before your time,' my grandmother would have offered. Or something about 'no point looking back', or maybe just 'least said'.

The solicitor didn't wear spectacles. He had no rim to peer over and frown, but his face crumpled into a grimace all the same.

'Your grandmother,' he coughed, 'she didn't make a will. Now, that's no problem in the ordinary way of things. Your parents are dead you say, so you would inherit if there are no other closer relations. But that's the thing. I can't find any evidence of your existence. No birth certificate. None for a mother either. There's no record that your grandmother …' that cough again … 'ever had a child for that matter. You are a bit of a puzzle my dear and the way things stand, there's no way you can inherit. I've done my best, but there's a second cousin, twice removed, who is making a claim.'

I opened my mouth. I tried to say about five and three, but the numbers stuck behind my teeth.

'She rented the land out to a farmer, but it was hers along with the house. She always said it would be mine one day. The moor, beyond, it's important … I'm sixteen … I'm old enough to look after it …'

He patted my hand. He patted my back. He wanted to help, but his hands were tied. 'It's impossible to sort the paperwork out.' He offered to put me in touch with someone in Social Services. He mentioned adoption records or a private detective.

'I'm sorry,' he said.

Not as sorry as me, but Grandmother had always told me not to cry once the milk was spilled. I could picture her mouth puckering, 'Get a cloth and mop it up!'

There was money under the mattress. A foolish place, but there had been no telling her that. Right at the bottom was one piece of newspaper about five inches square, folded into three. I read it twice before I filled a suitcase. I combed my hair. I put a hairgrip in place. I carried all my drawings in a plastic bag. The solicitor was busy, but his secretary took me to a room and sat me down. She was old enough to have grey hair and her eyes didn't flicker at the sight of a kilt on a teenage girl, held fast with a safety pin.

I told her about the door and the numbers: how five went out and three came back. I'd always known that two were lost, but who were the other three? They must be alive? Surely someone could explain. I needed help. I needed to know who to ask.

She rolled a pen around between finger and thumb.

'I know that story,' she said at last. 'But it wasn't your mother. No, this goes back much further than that. My own mother told it to me. It was your grandmother I'm sure. Her mother died of a fever.' The secretary touched the tips of her fingers and counted back. 'They were hard times. And people were afraid. Her mother wasn't welcome in the churchyard. A fever like that could sweep through a place. There were three volunteers and your grandmother's father. Coffins were expensive ...'

Grandmother had tied my tongue with a rope of rules hung with fives and threes. If I'd asked sooner, would someone have told me?

They carried her up to the black peat tops. They found a pool that was deep enough to place her in. They weighted her feet with stones carried up in deep pockets. They circled her neck with an iron chain. They dropped her in, but her hands floated up to the surface like lilies … The words took life and painted a death. I could see it all. Her husband threw himself in. Three men came back and each had a different tale: he loved her too much to let her go into the bog alone; he was trying to weight the hands down; he slipped. They tried to save him, so the telling went, but the soft earth sucked and they were afraid to go in.

Grandmother was small at the time. She was sent away to be raised by some relative. The house was rented out, then it stood empty for years. Some of the fixtures and fittings were stripped.

'When she came back, you came too. She kept herself to herself and you along with her. No one knows about her life for the years in between.'

The attendant is kind. She sits by my side and asks if *The Lady of Shalott* holds some special meaning for me, or if I just like its beauty. Her hand lies on my arm. Perfume rises up from her wrist. For a moment it pulls at a memory until I remember that 'a hand that stirs myrtle like incense' isn't mine to claim.

'Are you all right?' The attendant asks. 'I'm due a break in a minute. I have a flask of coffee and two cups. We could sit on a bench in the sun.'

She squeezes my arm. 'Don't be afraid to look at the world outside, whatever it holds.'

The back of my eyes prickles with pins. When there are enough little holes the tears will flow. Like a wave. Like a torrent. Like an anguished call. I want to tell her about five and three. I want to let words tumble out like the balm of ointment on a chest on a cold winter night. I want to imagine her arm is as loving as my grandmother's as it circles me and keeps me safe.

The newspaper cutting gave me a name. It gave me a face with a high forehead and a clump of fringe pushed up in a cow's lick. Grandmother stole me away. I was never hers, but she took me anyway. She tried to change her past by making it mine.

'But you can't do that!' I bleat the words out.

'I'm sorry. I just wanted to help.' The attendant stands. Her cheek is pink, as if it's been slapped.

'No! That's not what I mean …'

I stare at the ground. Her heels must make her feet ache, but at least they don't tap away across the floor. She waits to hear what I might say.

We all have our own tale, whether it's spoken aloud or hidden inside.

My mother had a job interview. She left me in a pram by the door. I had a biscuit and a bottle of milk. There were straps. The brake was on. She was a single mother: the reporter was against her for that.

There's a photograph with hands at the side of her face. The eyes are closed and puffed with tears. There are words printed out that must have fallen from her open mouth. They run in straight lines across the page, but I'm sure they must have jumped and dribbled, gasped and wailed: a thousand sheep calling for a thousand lambs have taught me how loss sounds.

'I didn't know what to do. I couldn't bring her in with me. I didn't know. I thought that the sort of people who come to a gallery would be all right. Please find my baby. Don't harm her. Please give her back safe to me ...'

There's a crease across the printed face and the black and white has faded to browner shades with time.

I wonder if they gave her the job and kept her here for all these years because of what happened. Maybe they were just being kind. Or maybe my mother loves art as much as I do and the pictures replaced me in her life. In a plastic bag I have a hundred sketches for a painting of a woman in white, but I have to be brave. I need to raise my head and look closer to know the colour of her eyes.

The heels don't move away. The legs are meshed in black. A belt cinches a waist as narrow as mine. A hand holds the beat in place beneath a soft blouse. Her name cries out from an embossed badge. Her neck. Her lips … cheek … eyes. Blue!

'Do you believe in fairy tales?' I ask.

ROSE PETAL BLUES

I don't know why some people live to be a hundred and others stop breathing before they've even had one birthday. I don't know why some people splat a spider without really thinking and others rescue the big hairy ones from the bottom of the bath. I don't know why I should have survived past my eleventh birthday or what right I had to expect to grow love instead of fear.

My little sister is called Lettie. Her job is to cut and clean bamboo. She would have loved a pet lamb to feed and would have tended a broody hen, or collected eggs without any reminder. I suspect she would have fed calves from a bucket and even milked a cow if her hands were big enough, but there are no animals on our farm.

We live back in the hills, in a fertile cleft with great shelter from northerly winds. A stream of sharp, clear water runs right through the middle of our yard. We use this for washing and drinking. We use it for the long hours of watering when the summer sun has frightened the clouds enough to make a drought.

Eena is our mother. We've never called her that, but I think she must be. Other people say, 'How's your mother keeping, Mary Ann?'

I always say, 'Fine'. Not 'Mother's fine', or 'Eena's fine' or even 'She's fine', for that matter. Words can be dangerous things.

Eena's job is to bind the bamboo together to make trellises. She also makes skeletons of wigwams and arches. These were her 'big selling line' for a few years, but she always had other ideas. Lately the trellises have been neglected, but Lettie still has to cut and stack the bamboo: 'It's a fall-back position,' Eena says.

My job is to pick rose petals. Eena doesn't take much notice of what we do, as long as the jobs are finished each day.

Some roses are bred for looks and a few are bred for scent, but there is more theft than breeding in the ones that grow around the farmyard. Eena calls it conservation, or rescuing of rare breeds, but in truth, she simply stole the first rose. A cutting wasn't enough. She dug up the whole thing. Admittedly the owner was old and rather deaf, which was why she could clatter around with her spade and not be found out. Eena has green fingers and large grey areas of conscience.

She planted the rose and clipped cuttings from it, until I doubted it would live. The rose thrived. It grew snakes of twining green in the first year and each cutting burst out healthy leaves. Eena planted an avenue, an arbour and draped the walls of the house. Thorns multiplied.

It's always hard to tell if there is a plan in Eena's life. Some projects seem organised, others just unfold due to circumstance. The roses flourish and expand ecstatically to a plan of nature, but Eena wants to dictate the end result.

Some roses have names that conjure exotic images: moyesii, bourboniana, floribunda, spinosissima. Eena's was just 'her' rose, but it became mine. Each flower had a double ring of ballroom-dance-dress-pink petals; a barbed stem with thorns set so close there was no place to rest an idle finger; and the most heady, thick scent, that rolled with notions of indolence. I choose the last word carefully, for notions are important things.

This summer Eena pronounced the roses 'ready' and I was told to pick. The first week my fingers bled.

'Like Snow White,' Eena said and licked a drop from a perfect petal.

I know enough of fairy tales to know it was Sleeping Beauty who pricked her finger. I know about Wicked Stepmothers and Handsome Princes: even rose-petal-pickers have to attend some school. Even bamboo cutters hear a few fairy tales.

This summer I filled a basket with petals, then another, then another. We made piles of petals in the attic so that the baskets were free for filling again and again. My fingers have hardened. The tips can take the kiss of thorns without flinching. Eena has begun to brew. She boils and stirs. She adds drops from small bottles and distils heady scents through long copper coils. I pick to feed the monster, and the scent of rose goes beyond the farmyard. It seeps into the fabric of the house. It soaks into my hands. It steals into the water that we drink. I breathe it in and breathe out the few remaining drops of me that are not yet rose.

Eena calls her bottles 'Perfume from Paradise'.

When we leave the farm, all squashed along the front seat to make room for the bottles in the back, we don't notice that the car is full of the richness of rose petal. When we arrive in town and set up a rickety table with a hand-painted sign, we don't comment on the number of people who look our way. We are used to looking a little different: too many bright colours in a sea of grey suits and black coats. It's only when I wander off to buy tape to stick the sign to the table, that I begin to wonder why people sniff the air, why they turn and follow me.

Eena loves a crowd. She sparkles with the attention. She waves a long silk scarf of deepest red, shot with silver. She chants in a singsong about the exotic perfume: its passion, its perfection, its purity, its price. Lettie sits on a stone step watching. She pulls her fingers through tangled hair.

Eena sells every single bottle and even then people don't move away until we leave. She pronounces the day 'a great success' and clutches her purse with one hand while she drives with the other. Lettie and I take turns to jerk the gear stick from point to point, as Eena shouts the numbers aloud.

Now, bamboo can be forgotten. We all stir the pot, or fill the bottles, or write the labels and apply the glue. I am still the one to pick the petals. They never seem to lessen although I pick and pick and the year is moving on.

Eena decides that the second batch of bottles should be brought to the city. We set up our pitch outside the door of an expensive department store. The table looks shabby. Lettie is almost curled in on herself with embarrassment. I wish we could have left her at home, but Eena insisted. This time I am more prepared. I notice the effect on the passers-by.

Eena still seems to think it's her performance that attracts the crowd, so to make the point I move off a little, up the street. The crowd moves with me. Some people play music to charm rats. Others exude perfume. I'm not sure which one I would rather be.

It's true that you never notice how you smell yourself. But having said that, I've never really got used to the smell of rose petals. It taints the food I eat and the dreams I escape to. Every time I move, a ripple of perfume moves with me.

'The people are charmed,' Eena says, as I struggle to hit fourth gear on our way home. She doesn't mean they like me. She's just working things out.

Lots of people wonder what it's like to be a guinea pig, but few speculate about being the bait in a trap. I get first-hand experience.

The magic is this: I have absorbed so much 'roseness', from a rose of such incredible perfume, that I exude it in my sweat, in my breath and in my piss. I only have to move an arm and a heady swirl pulses from me.

The next bit of magic is this: the people who inhale my perfume are drawn into memories as deep as a race can hold. They feel sensuous, they feel passionate, they feel loved, cherished and supported, they feel powerful in a way that the hunter feels before he strikes, they feel the touch of divinity. They buy the perfume.

The human touch is this: Eena wants to bottle my secretions. She stokes the fire and feeds me orange juice.

Lettie returns, of her own accord, to stacking bamboo. I try to talk to her but she moves a few paces away. 'I want things back the way they were,' she says.

Things weren't good before, so I worry.

'Everything could get better,' I say. 'We can make more money.'

'Money will make no difference,' she says. 'You wait and see.'

Lettie is often right about things. I do wait. I expect I will see.

'You stink,' she adds as she walks away holding her nose.

Eena buys me a new dress. She buys Lettie a hat. We visit offices in tall buildings with glass that I feel like flying through, and views of the sky that say I don't need to bother. People shake my hand. They sniff at the bottles offered by Eena. Their eyes go mushy and they hold themselves more loosely. They shuffle papers. We leave, to return another day.

Lettie and I have been sworn to secrecy. On no account can we tell how we make the perfume. I'm not sure what I would say if anyone did ask and Lettie, for sure, would be too embarrassed to tell.

Eena is afraid I will lose the power. She makes me walk through the roses and makes Lettie rub my bare skin with crushed petals, but I am confused. I used to long for an ordinary life. I wanted chicken nuggets for tea and cornflakes for breakfast. I wanted television and hot baths. Believe me, I knew what I had been missing. Eena could cook porridge and asafoetida pancakes. She could make carrageen soup and slippery elm shakes. She could cast a horoscope and hand-felt slippers. But she can't raise children: not the right way. I am sure about that.

We return to the tall buildings and meet with lawyers and advertisers, with promoters and directors. Eena signs her name to papers and tries to make me sign mine, but I do it a different way each time. We go to lunches where no nuggets are on the menu. We trail behind Eena like two little ducks. She was the first thing imprinted on our memories. What other back can we waddle behind?

Eena gets catalogues on jacuzzis, but she still makes us drink down the bitter dregs of feverfew tea. At night, in bed, Lettie comes to cuddle up close.

'You smell different today,' she says.

How many more meetings? I don't know. There has been a change, only no one has noticed. Lettie and I whisper in bed. The first contracts were torn up. Everyone wanted more profit, more bottles, bigger promotion. As I passed two men on the street they started to fight. Children burst into tears demanding more sweets, more ice-cream.

'You really smell odd,' Lettie laughs. 'The roses are fading. You smell like dirty money and greasy handshakes.'

Does the perfume of greed sell well?

The next bit of magic is this: I've been exposed to too many selfish people of late. In truth, I'm a little afraid. Roses can't hide all smells.

The last bit of magic is this: I still know what I truly want.

If things go badly wrong – and I know they will, because the flowers are almost all gone on the roses outside, and the smell of the gutter and coins in a beggar's cap gets stronger each day – we will still have bamboo trellises. We could sell rose cuttings to twine through their squares. There isn't much time.

I try for a while, to absorb the cool scent of the wild water flowing through the yard. I roll in damp grass in the hope that something will cling, but I realise that all this is pointless. There is one thing I want. One chance only, of making things work out for Lettie and me.

I make friends with children called Eva and Grace. I visit their home as often as I can. This is no idle choice. I've walked the streets and figured out who bakes every day. I know the smells of stew and apple pie, of cooking marshmallows, hot chocolate and warm bread. 'These are the scents I am working on,' I tell Lettie. 'This is our chance to make it right.' She smiles and strokes the back of my hand.

I don't imagine people want a perfume of chocolate cake, or that they want a room freshener of chicken nuggets, but that isn't my plan. I sit as close to Eena as I can. I wave my arms when asking her to pass things and I rub the back of her neck when she gets angry at the letter from the lawyers and promoters, cancelling all hope of a perfume empire.

I don't imagine for a moment that she will become a new person overnight. I don't imagine that she will become like Eva and Grace's mother, but I do see a change. Tonight she cooked a chicken for tea and produced a pot of homemade yoghurt for desert. She even noticed that Lettie has grown out of her nightdress.

I watched the last petal fall from the roses today, but I didn't need to catch its dying fragrance. I held Lettie's hand. We don't want to distil another perfume. We have other plans. If Eena can absorb some small bit of the scent of biscuits, hugs and bedtime stories, we'll be just fine. All we want is the magic of an ordinary life.

WALKING BACKWARDS

'If you knew that you were going to die tomorrow, what would you do today?'

Lissy turned a shoulder, to get closer, as if she had a right to ask.

The number 21B shook when it stopped and rattled when it moved. It leapt forward with a jolt, sending an old man and his tartan shopping bag into a trot-along quickstep towards the back.

'What?'

The young man sitting next to her was too big for the seat. He spread sideways. His arm pushed into Lissy, even though she'd tried to help by squashing herself right up to the window. She'd turned her back for the first two hops between stops, but he hadn't got off and his arm had spread further into her seat. He made it hard to concentrate.

Lissy pushed her lips close to the glass and puffed out a breath. It came back to her face in a part-warmed, part-cooled tumble of air. The window clouded over. Her finger tapped against it and left a round dot. What would she want to see instead of city streets? A house with four windows and a door?

A tree full of apples? A happy family? None of her pictures could offer up the answer, so she'd decided to ask the fat man.

She could tell by his expression that he wanted to ignore her, but he was caught off-guard by her round smiling face with its blue-eyed, blonde crop and dimple to one side. His eyes flicked with thoughts: sweet seven, or eight, or nine, or ten? She was small for her age and grown-ups could never guess right.

'I was just wondering,' she said. 'If you were an old man like that.' She tipped her head carefully so it didn't collide with his coat. 'What if you were told that you would die tomorrow? What would you do with your last day alive?'

The fat man shuffled his bum in the narrow seat. His belly wobbled like waves in a goldfish bowl, sloshing from side to side. Lissy had a goldfish once, and a bowl, and waves that sloshed until the fish fell out and died. It had been an experiment. She'd learned that fish can't live without water and that if things slosh too much, something might die.

'Do I know you?' he asked. 'Didn't your mother tell you not to talk to strangers?'

She shook her head and smiled. He wasn't such an old grown-up: more a big boy. A very, very big boy. One who was squashed too close to her side.

'I've got a girlfriend,' he added, as he tried to stand and squeeze free.

His breath pumped out in fast little snorts. He waited for the bus to stop, for the door to open, before glancing back with a frown on his forehead. Lissy spread her arms out across the two seats. She'd paid for a whole one and had only used half for most of the time.

Maybe the boy was thinking about his girlfriend and how he would spend a last day on earth if he could. He'd probably want to kiss all day. Grown-ups liked to kiss. Lissy knew that, because her mum had told her. It was after Lissy walked into the kitchen for a glass of water and found her mum kissing a man by the back door. She didn't know who the man was, but she was sure that you should never kiss strangers, even if talking to them might be all right. She'd tried kissing the glass, kissing her fingers, kissing her arm, but she couldn't see what there was to like.

Lissy wondered whether to talk to the old man on the seat behind. She could turn and ask what he would do if it was his last day alive. The man was so old that this really might be his last day. In which case, he was doing no better than Lissy: just riding on a bus as if a last day was no different from any other. As if riding on a bus was a good way to finish up a life.

Lissy's mum stood by the mirror. She tapped at her hair with the tips of her fingers, trying to get each strand right. The fumes from the hairspray caught in her throat, making her cough. Curls twirled and bounced back in perfect loops. They mostly stayed where she wanted, when she shook her head from side to side. The lapels of her coat lay flat, squashing down a white collar with a frill of lace. She ran a hand across a shoulder and gave a quick flick to brush away imaginary flakes.

The kitchen table was littered with crumbs. She glanced at the clock. A crust of bread lay drying on a board. A knife dripped jam on a flower-patterned plate.

There'd been a letter from school about healthy lunches. It praised apples and yoghurts. Lissy's mum swore she would buy some, but it was hard to find time. It didn't help that Lissy distracted and asked foolish questions while breakfast ticked by.

Like: Why do you have to work, Mum? You never used to!

Or: Why can't you be here when I get home from school?

Or: Did his tongue taste yucky? Was he trying to push it in your mouth?

Or, worst of all: Why can't things be the same as they were before?

Lissy's mum flicked back the lid of a phone. Her finger tapped over the keys: 'I'm on my way ... Right ... Twenty minutes if the traffic is good ... Bye, bye, bye.'

She got into the car the right way: bum down, knees together and swing. There was dirt on the sill, but it didn't touch her tights and her slim heels lifted on over. The traffic was terrible. Twenty minutes were more like thirty as she turned into the hotel car park, switched off the engine and pulled out the key. The phone rang.

'I'm here ... Sorry. No, I didn't change my mind. It was backed up all along the canal ... I know. I know. But I had to get my daughter off to the bus ... You saw her! Remember? We've hours now till she's back from school. I'll be up in a minute ... Of course I've got the bag. Trust me, I look the part.'

Her heels tip-tapped towards the building. A black computer case hung from her shoulder as she stepped round in time to a door that revolved slowly, pulling her inside.

The 21B was the most boring bus route. It went round in a loop: *Train Station, City Centre, School, Bus Station, End of Lissy's Road, Canal Bridge, Train Station* and so on. If Lissy got on early in the morning, when the bus was full, she could sometimes do three loops before the driver noticed and made her get off at the school. Some days she wore a disguise. The driver laughed once, when she wore thick glasses and a plastic nose, but he usually ignored a wrapped-around scarf. That suited her fine. She was working on becoming transparent: clear as glass. So no one could see her, or the things that ticked and sloshed inside.

She pulled a hat from her pocket. It had two flaps that came down over her ears and was as soft as a kitten. Kittens weren't pink, she knew that, but if she shut her eyes and stroked, she could imagine that the soft fluff was a black and white, or a tortoiseshell curled beneath her fingers. In her head she could hear the exact noise that a hat-cat would make. It was somewhere between a purr and a loving meow. There were two long strings that could fasten under her chin. She didn't like to tie them. It made her look even younger if the hat was held on with a bow.

'Actually I'm ten,' she said to the old man as she slid across the seat.

He was busy mopping his nose and didn't lift his head to reply.

Lissy left the bus halfway through the first loop. *City Centre* came before *School*. It was part of her plan. *City Centre* had happy people. *City Centre* had warm shops. *City Centre* didn't ask about homework, or if she could spell Mississippi with the right number of Ss and Ps.

There was a man stretched in a doorway, sleeping. Lissy bent and whispered in his ear: 'The world might end tomorrow.'

He rumbled up with a hand held out. Lissy took a step backward, almost tripping over a string and a small dog, but she didn't run.

'What would you do with today?'

'Feck off.'
So she did.

Lissy's mum stepped through the lobby and avoided the desk. 'Keep a purposeful look,' he'd told her. Her eyes were fixed on the door to the lift. It was around to the right, past a row of marble columns that looked as if the Parthenon had been lifted up and plonked down inside a hotel. That's what he'd told her, as well as how much he loved the wave of her ass when she walked in front and he stood behind.

'Wave it right on into the lift and head up to the top floor,' he'd said. 'If anyone asks, you're my secretary. You've got papers for me to sign. Have you got that?'

She knew that no one would ask. He just liked the thrill of thinking that they might.

Lissy hadn't asked her mum what she would do with her last day alive, because she already knew the answer: her mum would glue her mobile phone to one ear with super glue. It wouldn't matter, because she wouldn't need to sleep. That way she could talk, talk, talk, for a whole day and a whole night. Her mum would know what she wanted to do with a last day, no problem. She'd go all giggly and blow kisses into the phone when she thought Lissy couldn't hear. It was no good asking her mum. She'd have no idea what Lissy should do. Same as she had no idea what Lissy ever did. Same as she looked right through Lissy and didn't see what moved inside.

It was easy to skip school. Lissy ate three Mars bars and stalked a tall, blond boy with a tattoo on one arm. She stepped forward and back twenty-nine times, making the automatic doors to a shop open and shut, open and shut, open and shut, before she was asked to stop.

'Well my day was great,' she said to the man who slept in a doorway. The dog sniffed her leg.

'Spare a bit of change?' the man replied.

Lissy did one and a half loops on the bus. The driver didn't notice and she got to stare at the canal bridge as they drove by.

Lissy's mum lay on the bed. It was extra large, maybe twice the size of a normal divan. Super king-sized, he called it with a curl of his lip. The maid's uniform was too tight at the waist. A garter ruffled at the top of her thigh, but it didn't hide the beginnings of cellulite. Her belly was covered with stretch marks spattered in silver lines. The computer case lay open on a table. He took the handcuffs and the gag from inside.

Lissy's mum wasn't sure if this was such a good idea. She wasn't sure if she liked 'stepping things up a notch', or 'keeping it quiet to add to the thrill'. Why was he fully dressed anyway, while she lay like a fresh-plucked turkey? And why did 'sage and onion' keep popping into her mind?

Was it just loneliness that had led her here? She blamed her lips that couldn't stop kissing when he came up behind her in the photocopy room, or when he followed her home and slid a hand under her blouse on the doorstep. Or maybe it was his voice on the end of the phone, talking dirty until her lips slackened and her heart beat fast. Or maybe her wiggling ass should take all the blame.

What if he changed his mind when he noticed the stretch marks? What if her body didn't live up to the dream? What if she'd forgotten how to please a man?

Instead, Lissy's mum forgot that she was Lissy's mum, while she panted and posed and closed her eyes. Her boss had fantasies of maids and ties. Hers was of twelve years past, when she'd lain in the arms of a husband who'd sworn to love her for all of his life.

Lissy pushed open the front door. She'd had a key of her own for a year or so. It was attached to the ring on her pencil case. One time, the pencils had all fallen out as she opened the door. That was because she hadn't zipped the case up properly after Geography, or was it Maths? No fear of that happening again.

Lissy had missed Geography, and Maths as well. She'd also missed break time, where the children shouted: 'Pissy Lissy, Pissy Lissy. Can't spell Mississippi,' when she walked by.

Her mum wasn't home. She never got back before half five or six. Lissy spread some jam on the crust that curled on the table, then licked it all off because the crust was too hard. She went up to her room and lay on her bed, with her feet dangling over the edge. The bed was too small, but Lissy liked it that way. She picked up a photograph and kissed the glass. It was as dead as kissing her arm. She stared into the smiling eyes. The glow-in-the-dark stars began to shine on the ceiling, as the day let go of its share of light.

Lissy's mum stared up at the light fitting. Her arms were above her head. She tried to look at her watch, but the face was turned away. Her shoulders ached.

'Stay for the night,' he said.

'I can't. There's my daughter. I told you about her,' she replied. She wanted to ask if she would still be paid for the day and how that would work. Was it sick pay from the office, or, if he paid her in cash, would that be sicker still?

'Give her a call. Tell her you'll be late,' he said. He freed her wrists. She flicked open the phone. Her finger flew over the keys.

'There's pizza in the freezer. I won't be too late. Lock the door if you're going to bed,' she said.

There was a half second of silence, before a rattle of words flew out to her ear: 'IF THIS WAS YOUR ABSOLUTELY LAST DAY, LAST EVENING, LAST OF EVERYTHING, BECAUSE YOU'D BE STONE DEAD TOMORROW, WOULD YOU STILL GO OUT WITH HIM? WOULD YOU FORGET ABOUT DAD?'

The man heard the words too, but he just touched his hand to his hair and smiled back from the mirror.

'Oh Lissy!' Mum said. 'I'm running a bit late is all. I'll be there before midnight, sooner, maybe. Remember the door, Lissy. Remember the door.'

'That's all right then,' the man said, as he ran a finger over her arm and back.

Lissy's mum knew that it wasn't. That everything was far from right, but her voice was stuck behind bright red lips, that were too tangled up with kisses and licks to shape a reply.

Lissy looked through the window. *Almost there* she said to her-self as she stroked the glass. She looked down at her jumper. It was hard to tell, but if she lifted the layers and stared at her belly where it curved in a mound with the belly button tucked like a dimple on top; if she looked hard until her eyes watered, or, if she squinted a bit with one eye and shut the other, then maybe, just maybe, it all went fuzzy enough for her to see right down to the guts and the kidneys and the tubes full of poo. But tears got in the way. It was hard to see clearly and there was no one to ask what they could see inside.

Outside, the evening was black above the street lamps and Lissy was scared of the dark. Every light in the house was switched on. Even the pink one with tassels by the bed in her mum's room, but there were still dark corners: Lissy did her best to avoid those. She ate a Pop-Tart in the fluorescent-lit kitchen. She looked at a photo album under the anglepoise on the desk in the sitting room. There was no point in watching TV: that wasn't a last day sort of thing. The box blared anyway, if just for the sound of a voice and an extra square of light. Lissy looked back at the dark above the street lamps. It stretched up and up.

Maybe last days should be about squashing down fears. At least then she would have done something. Maybe last days should be about going out at night like a grown-up and seeing what all the fuss was about.

The pink hat made her face look even rounder as she stepped out of the house, leaving the door unlocked behind her. She didn't want to bring her pencil case and didn't think to slip the key free.

There was a different driver on the night-time bus. He took her money and didn't smile. She sat at the back and watched people get on and off, but no one sat beside her, or pressed too close. They passed *Canal Bridge* and *Train Station*. She stood up at *City Centre* and joined the push to get off.

'Can I sit in your doorway?' She asked the man with the dog. He sipped from a bottle and spread a hand so the fingers stretched out.

'You want to know what I'd do if there was no tomorrow?'

Lissy smiled. He'd remembered! She nodded her head up and down. The pink hat slipped further over her brow.

'Come on,' he said. 'I'll show you. Hold my hand.'

The dog hopped along at his side.

'That was fun,' the boss said. He packed up the bag and shut down the lid.

'I don't want to do this again!' Lissy's mum replied.

'That's up to you,' he smiled. 'You seemed to enjoy it.'

He raised her hand to his lips and licked with a flick of a tongue across the cuticles, below the painted nails.

'I haven't touched a man since my husband died,' she said. 'I needed to try something different. I thought if I did, it wouldn't remind me of him.'

'Oh,' he said. 'I didn't know.' He raised an eyebrow and glanced at his watch at the same time.

'It was a year ago. Cancer.'

'Really?' He moved towards the door, straightening his tie.
'My job?' she asked.

'I won't fire you, if that's what you mean. Look around at
the other girls. You're not the first and you won't be the last. No
one will think less of you than they do of themselves.' He lifted
the edge of his lips in a crooked smile.

Lissy's mum kept her head down as she walked past the
columns in the lobby. 'Tragedy' and 'ruins' were the words that
flashed through her mind. Her boss threw a key onto the desk
at reception, but didn't glance her way or hold her hand in his.

He'd flirted for weeks. He'd followed her home. Then this.
She'd giggled and groped as if she was still a girl, instead of
someone grasping the past with fingers that couldn't hold
tight. Like someone twelve years younger, who didn't have a
child to mind.

She sat into her car, bum first, knees together, and lifted her
heels over the dirt on the sill. Rain blew along the canal and
the streets were quiet. The lights by the bridge were against her.
She sat waiting, holding her breath and wondering how she
could pull some joy back into her life.

Out of the corner of her eye she could see a man, perched
on the side of the bridge. He had a pink hat on his head that
was just like Lissy's. Rain dripped from the end of the strings
that weren't tied. He hopped off the wall and came towards the
window. His thin hand knocked twice.

'IF THIS WAS THE LAST DAY OF YOUR LIFE, WHAT WOULD YOU DO?' he shouted.

Her eyes locked on the red light. Her hands gripped the wheel.

'I'LL TELL YOU,' he roared. 'YOU'D HOLD YOUR DAUGHTER TIGHT, SO SHE DIDN'T SLIP FREE AND SHATTER LIKE GLASS!'

Lissy's mum opened her mouth in a round and looked straight at him. No words came out. She saw him stagger. His face was covered in tears beneath the pink hat. Her foot slipped out the clutch as something crawled in her belly and threatened to creep out of her throat. She sped forward along the road by the high canal. The man, whose home was a door-way, watched her drive away. He sat back on the wall with his face turned up to the darkness above the street lamps.

'This is for Lissy,' he cried.

Lissy's arms were stretched wide. She floated. It was later, much later, after a man held her hand. He was a nice man. He'd understood that sometimes you have to walk backwards to get where you're going. They'd stood on the canal bridge and looked at the water that was high along the edges.

'I might jump in,' Lissy said.

'I might too,' he'd replied.

That was after they'd looked in the windows of houses and

restaurants. He'd shown her people eating at tables and sipping on wine.

'That's what I'd do,' he said. 'If it was my last day and I could do anything I wanted. I'd step backwards, into the life that was there before I lost everything. I'd eat a real meal, at a clean table. I'd drink wine and stop before the bottle was empty.'

'That's easy,' Lissy laughed. They walked backwards all the way to her house and they stepped back in through the open door.

'Walking backwards turns back time,' she said. 'I do it lots, but I never get back to before Dad died.'

She'd shown him the bed that her dad had made, when she was small enough to be lost in its size. She'd shown him the picture of her mum smiling in her white wedding dress. She'd told him that *before* was sometimes too far back to find. They'd eaten pizza and Lissy had poured him one glass of wine from the bottle in the fridge.

'Can you see through me?' she'd asked. He'd listened to her wish to become clear as glass. He didn't laugh.

'I can,' he'd answered. 'I can see right into the middle. Past the titties that haven't grown. Past the pizza that's churning around. I can see a sad girl with a bad mum, but that's a long way from where I am in my life.'

They'd made a trade and shaken hands. Then they'd made

another. She'd given her hat for his dog. He'd looked silly, but that was all right, because she'd told him it was a cat-hat and he'd said that they have nine lives. The dog hadn't stayed. It wriggled and barked in her arms, then ran off behind him as soon as he walked round the corner at the end of the street.

Lissy's mum stood in the bedroom looking down at her sleeping child. The covers were thrown back. Lissy's arms were stretched wide, waiting for someone to hug.

'I'm sorry. Really, I'm sorry,' Lissy's mum said.

She climbed onto the small bed and wrapped an arm across Lissy's chest.

'Mmmm,' Lissy mumbled. 'Toughened glass is a special sort. It doesn't break, so that's all right. And I want a puppy if I'm staying alive.'

'Hush now. Night-night. Mind the bed bugs don't bite.' Lissy's mum pushed her lips into blonde, cropped hair and breathed in the familiar scent of her child.

'If this was my last day,' she whispered. 'I'd spend it holding you.'

Lissy's friend, in the pink hat, tied his dog to a lamppost. He sat on the bridge and felt good inside. He'd not harmed the child. He'd eaten a last supper and drunk one glass of wine: like a fine man in a healthy life. He'd not taken anything from the house and had only shouted when he recognised the woman in the car, waiting at the lights. It was the best day in a long time. A high note! A bit like the one that rang from his lips as he tipped backwards into the water. The hat floated loose and he went down like a stone, but less hard, less flinty and more fluid at the core.

A trade is a trade, he thought as his lungs filled. *A deal is a deal*. He knew that he wasn't as lucky as a cat-hat. He knew that human beings only get one life.

AUTHOR'S NOTE

Short stories are the lift in my heart as I weed the garden and the beat in my brain as I walk the mountain thinking about opening sentences and plot twists. I love to tweak all the links and devices that tease a story from the head to make it live on the page. Sometimes stories fall out complete. Sometimes I agonise. That's the writer's lot it seems. But the writer's delight, the thrill that sends a shiver from head to toe and back again, is to see their stories published as a collection – babies swaddled between paper sheets.

ACKNOWLEDGEMENTS

I'd like to thank all the people who made this book possible: the ones who listened, read and encouraged, the ones who said 'don't give up', the ones who awarded prizes and the ones who helped a chain of events fall into place. The list is long and they know who they are, but in case they have forgotten, I'd like to mention a few:

Ben, Nick, Sam, Fi, Anna and Dave, who will always tell me my stories are great, because that's what family does. And Corin of course, who I'm sure will do the same once he is big enough.

Brídín, Meredith, Gloria, Sunny, Christine and Gana, who as friends and supporters have never stopped urging me on.

Pat Cotter for his encouragement and practical interventions.

And all at Mercier Press for putting their expertise and enthusiasm into the publishing of this book.

Grateful thanks to the following publications and competitions:

We All Fall Down won the Sean O'Faolain Short Story Competition 2006 and was first published in *Southword* 11.

Changes of Light won the Real Writers Short Story Competition International Award and was first published in *Real Writers* 2004.

High Nellie and the Far Horizon, *Blood Red* and *Crying for Worms*, won the START Chapbook Prize and were first published as same in 2004.

Knocking Down the Nails was shortlisted for the Sean O'Faolain Short Story Competition 2005 and was first published in *Southword* 9.

Fishing for Dreams won the RTÉ Francis MacManus Short Story Award 2010 and was first broadcast on RTÉ radio in 2011.

Precious Little was shortlisted for the Bridport Prize 2009.

Least Said and *Walking Backwards* were shortlisted for the Fish Short Story Competition 2011/2007, respectively.

Rose Petal Blues was Editor's Choice in the Fish Short Story Competition 2002 and was first published in *Franklin's Grace and Other Stories, Winners of Ireland's Fish Short Story Prize*.

Light, Thought and Evelyn was shortlisted in the Real Writers Short Story Competition 1999.

Also Available from Mercier Press

Short Stories

John B. Keane

978 1 85635 344 1

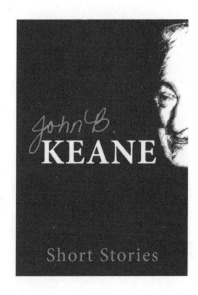

There are more shades to John B. Keane's humour than there are colours in the rainbow. Compassion, shrewdness and a glorious sense of fun and roguery are evident in this collection, which brings together John B. Keane's tales.

Included are gems such as 'The Hanging', a tale of accusation by silence in a small village, which shows both the comic and tragic effects of small-town gossip, and 'Guaranteed Pure', which concerns the innocence of bachelor Willie Ramley, who is seeking an unsullied bride in Ireland. Keen but never unkind, the attention of Ireland's best-loved writer falls on human vanities and frailties of all kinds.

www.mercierpress.ie

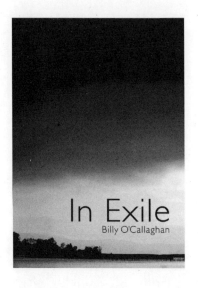

MERCIER PRESS

IRISH PUBLISHER - IRISH STORY

We hope you enjoyed this book.

Since 1944, Mercier Press has published books that have been critically important to Irish life and culture. Books that dealt with subjects that informed readers about Irish scholars, Irish writers, Irish history and Ireland's rich heritage.

We believe in the importance of providing accessible histories and cultural books for all readers and all who are interested in Irish cultural life.

Our website is the best place to find out more information about Mercier, our books, authors, news and the best deals on a wide variety of books. Mercier tracks the best prices for our books online and we seek to offer the best value to our customers, offering free delivery within Ireland.

Sign up on our website or complete and return the form below to receive updates and special offers.

www.mercierpress.ie
www.facebook.com/mercier.press
www.twitter.com/irishpublisher

Name: _____

Email: _____

Address: _____

Mobile No.: _____

Mercier Press, Unit 3b, Oak House, Bessboro Rd, Blackrock, Cork, Ireland